MW01274351

Belle of the Bayou is a comic fable which takes Arabella Slominski Boot on an odyssey to Lafayette, Louisiana in search of liberation.

Arabella is married to Roman Boot, a man who wears Listermint as cologne and thinks foreplay is a golf term. On her fortieth birthday Arabella catches Roman, naked save for a spiked dog collar, *in flagrante delicto* with her best friend Tanya. Arabella takes their son Kenny, and Roman's car and heads south to join Melva, a woman ranking high on the list of literature's most loathsome mothers.

As Arabella struggles towards independence she falls in love with an aging jazz musician Joe 'Hooty' Birmingham, a nomad who lives in the moment. But the path to romance is not smooth and Arabella's new life is beset by problems. Roman Boot, pressured by Tanya, sues for custody of Kenny. Kenny, much to Arabella's consternation, discovers girls. As she wails to a friend, 'Just a month ago he wouldn't have been able to pick a girl out of a line-up'. Melva is fired from her job. Arabella's stepfather dies, possibly assisted by the Liquid Plummer Melva has been adding to his milkshakes. And Arabella is stalked by a karate instructor the shape and density of a refrigerator.

But **Belle of the Bayou** *is* a comedy. Love conquers all and the book's ending promises sunshine and a brave new beginning.

Belle of the Bayou

Joanna Goodman

The Porcupine's Quill

CANADIAN CATALOGUING IN PUBLICATION DATA

Goodman, Joanna, 1969–
Belle of the bayou

ISBN 0-88984-198-5

I. Title.

PS8563.O8344B44 1998   C813'.54   C98-931434-0
PR9199.3.G66B44 1998

Published by The Porcupine's Quill,
68 Main Street, Erin, Ontario NOB 1TO.
Readied for the press by John Metcalf; copy edited by Doris Cowan.
Typeset in Galliard, printed on Zephyr Antique Laid,
and bound at the Porcupine's Quill Inc.

Cover photograph by Sherman Hines/Masterfile.

This is a work of fiction. Any resemblance of characters to persons,
living or dead, is purely coincidental.

Represented in Canada by the Literary Press Group.
Trade orders are available from General Distribution Services.

We acknowledge the support of the Ontario Arts Council,
and the Canada Council for the Arts for our publishing program.
The financial support of the Government of Canada
through the Book Publishing Industry Development Program
is also gratefully acknowledged.

1 2 3 4 • 00 99 98

For Miguel

A Magnificent Body

A WOMAN GETS ONE SHOT IN LIFE at turning forty; one single shot at acknowledging four decades of events which include menstruation, the excruciating loss of virginity, childbirth, child-rearing, menopause, and a propensity for carrying more fat cells. A woman's fortieth birthday is a turning point, an achievement that should be celebrated with accolades. And that's a shame, because for Arabella Slominski Boot the success or failure of her fortieth anniversary on earth hinged entirely on her husband – a man who uses Listermint mouthwash as cologne and thinks foreplay is a golf stroke.

Over a quiet dinner for two at the Bar-B-Barn, he handed her a single ticket for the 'Deep Space Nine' convention at the Holiday Inn (his dentist had had an extra.)

'Can you believe it?' Roman gushed. 'What are the chances?'

Arabella quietly tucked the ticket in her purse. 'I'm going alone?' she said.

'Dr Ootes only had the one ticket. But I don't mind dropping you off.'

'That's nice of you,' she said.

'You get to spend the whole day there, eight to six. And I'm sure they'll have a snack bar.'

'Roman,' she said. 'What is "Deep Space Nine"?'

'Oh, very funny, Ara.' And he laughed heartily at her sense of humour.

Oddly enough, the next day he came back to her with an alternative: one full day at a spa – Le Spa on fancy Laurier Street.

Arabella's eyes welled up. 'You mean instead of the "Space Nine" convention?' she cried jubilantly.

'You can still go to the convention if you want,' Roman told her. 'I'm just giving you another option.'

'I'll take the spa,' she said quickly, giving him back the 'Deep Space Nine' ticket. 'I want the spa.'

He shrugged, looking somewhat baffled. 'If that's your choice.... Maybe I can scalp the ticket.'

'I won't be hurt,' she said.

'You sure you prefer the spa?'

She nodded emphatically, giddily. He grabbed her rear end then, squeezing an ample handful of flesh, and said, 'I guess it'll do you some good. Maybe you'll get your old figure back.'

Her old figure. It would be a small miracle if one afternoon at Le Spa could restore the figure of her youth, could repair the damage of two children and hundreds of late night cartons of Häagen Dazs.

But what a figure it had been. Not many things went right for Arabella while she was growing up, but God surely blessed her with a magnificent body. It was the sort of body that gave a girl a bad reputation even if she didn't deserve one. Large breasts, high and firm, slender legs that never chafed, a tiny waist a man could wrap his hands around, and a tight round rear that swayed just right under her plaid school kilt. Funny thing was, Arabella was nothing but embarrassed by it. It was her stepfather, Cyrus – her mother's second husband – who first made her conscious of her body. He called her Ara-glass, for her shapely physique. Also, he had a wretched habit of barging into the bathroom whenever she was showering. Curiously, the door had a lock that was always broken. 'Ooops!' he'd say. 'I had no idea you were in here.'

Arabella often wondered what her real father – the man whose sperm had created her – would have been like. She wondered if he would have lied and leered the way Cyrus did. But her real daddy was dead, having been blown up in a pizza parlour in New York City. It happened when Arabella was one and as she got older she occasionally heard her mother whisper the word *Mafia* to anyone who would listen. So there was just no point in dwelling on what might have been – it was self-indulgent and futile. Cyrus was her father for as long as he stuck around, and as fate would have it, he stuck around long enough to impair her delicate pubescent self-esteem.

Instead of appreciating her splendid assets, Arabella slouched, stooped and slumped under dark baggy sweaters for the better part of high school. This was something her mother couldn't understand. 'Flaunt it!' her mother would say. 'Most women would kill for a set of hooters like yours.'

Her mother has always been short on sensitivity. She was hard and cold even before her first husband was blown up, and his violent death did little to soften her edges. Melva Cusper was as abrasive as a scouring pad on porcelain and she didn't look much better either. She was skinny as an X-ray and back then she sported a bleached white perm that frizzled at the edges like burnt shoelaces. While Arabella was growing up, Melva served beer at a topless bar on Ste. Catherine Street, the first of its kind in Montréal; this made her something of a pioneer in the field. She was prone to boasting about this, thought it gave her a slice of credibility as a woman. She wasn't exactly a raving beauty, so she picked up her self-worth wherever she could.

Melva was always shooting her mouth off like a cap gun – harmless and loud and irritating. Meanwhile Arabella was growing prettier and more voluptuous every year. Timid, cautious and apologetic, as though she didn't deserve to look so good and draw that kind of attention, to boys she was an enticing combination of modesty and unexplored sexuality. Her phone rang itself right off the hook with invitations to movies, concerts and dinners in expensive restaurants. But she always said, 'No, thank you.' She was polite about it, but firm. And then her mother, usually hovering nearby so she could listen in, would yelp, 'What is *wrong* with you?'

'They're just interested in one thing,' Arabella would explain. 'They don't really like *me*.'

'So what?' Melva always raged. 'So the hell what?'

But Arabella felt as if she had nothing to offer even the most unremarkable boys. She preferred steering clear of the humiliation, of the possibility that underneath that magnificent body lurked a dim-wit or a bore. And that way she avoided being called slutty, fast and easy; also being groped, fondled, probed and dumped.

Arabella's reclusiveness, particularly her disregard for the opposite sex, had Melva stumped and outright worried. 'There's something wrong with that girl,' she'd complain to Cyrus, loud enough for Arabella to hear. 'She's not a normal teenager.'

Arabella certainly couldn't argue with that; she *wasn't* normal. Never had been. Inside, she just didn't feel right about herself. She never felt good enough.

That's why when she was finally ready to fall in love, she was like a blinking Vacancy sign inviting anyone to come along and take advantage of her. She had no protective lining inside her, almost like a weak immune system, which left her susceptible to all sorts of negative forces.

In college, she majored in philosophy, which was open-ended and ambiguous. It suited her at the time for she often lost herself in the ambiguity. Intellectually, she could lurk in the shadows without ever having to commit herself. She managed to live her life without a solid thesis, both in college and out. By her second year, Arabella's mother had married a third time. The man, whose name was Nectar Spurnicky, was old – somewhere in his mid-sixties. His teeth made a clicking sound like tap shoes when he talked and there was a cork-coloured mole on his chin that always made Arabella faintly nauseous. But he had money. Enough to make the physical flaws nearly invisible. Sometimes if he spent enough cash on her, Melva told him he looked a little like Jimmy Stewart. He paid for a new house in Lafayette, Louisiana, a brand new 1974 Oldsmobile Cutlass Supreme, and he sent Arabella fifty dollars a week. He called it 'mad money' and she was grateful for it. She used it for matinees and records and paperback books with glossy pictures of women in low-cut dresses on the cover.

By twenty-one she had discovered a trick for squashing her breasts so that they all but disappeared; she bought brassieres two full sizes too small so her chest wound up looking as flat as a raft. Then she'd throw on a baggy black sweater and presto, she was incognito and asexual. She clung to her virginity even through the wild liberated late sixties and early seventies. Her mother, by now quite alarmed, rattled off a slew of insults every time Arabella went home for the holidays: spinster, old maid, prude, goody-two-shoes.

'How's the lesbo these days?' she once cackled.

But no matter what her mother said, Arabella would not be swayed over to the other side, to the dark and petrifying territory of the sexually active. She felt she could have stayed a virgin forever.

She hadn't counted on Eric Slominski. He was a professor at college, taught Polish history at the third and fourth year levels. He was middle-aged, lanky and completely graceless. He was too tall for himself, as though he just couldn't get comfortable with all that height. He was always hunching and he had enormous feet. There was a dishevelled beard on his chin that grew out in all directions and felt like guitar strings. His hair was brown and grey, like her mother's old beaver coat. He was no Warren Beatty but there was something she liked about him; maybe it was his safe droopy posture or the way his soft belly fell over his corduroys. He was physically unintimidating but then he caught her off guard with a quick wit and sharp intellect.

He took her to a café in the McGill ghetto and bought her cappuccinos. He made her laugh and it all seemed very artsy and sophisticated. She was used to instant coffee, black and bitter, and only when she studied late at night. Usually it was Sanka. The cappuccinos were like satin. Sometimes Eric puffed on a pipe, other times they shared a pack of Gauloises between them. Their conversations were as rich as the coffee. Eric was a genius – at least Arabella thought so. He knew all about art, wine and travel, and he read the *Globe and Mail*.

He liked to challenge her to political debates which she always lost – gladly. A favourite topic of his was René Lévesque's new PQ party. He referred to Bill 101 as the raping of English society, which she found boldly subversive. He devoured books and was always asking her if she had read such-and-such by so-and-so.

'Have you read Rousseau's *Social Contract*?' he'd ask, while the smoke of his cigarette obscured his face.

She'd shake her head, mute and intrigued.

'Do you ever wonder, Arabella, if certain humans are born evil or if they mutate under the exposure to society?'

Another ineffectual shake of her head, whereupon he would proceed to spew verbatim excerpts. 'I quote,' he would preface: '"Like the statue of Glaucus, which was so disfigured by time, seas and tempests, that it looked more like a wild beast than a god, the human soul, altered in society by a thousand causes perpetually recurring ... has, so to speak, changed in appearance, so as to be hardly recognizable."'

Here he would pause smugly for effect, waiting for her awestruck little face to react. When she said nothing, he would plod on. More quotes, pontifications and condemnations swirling around her dizzy head. 'Man,' he would declare, 'is the product of society! A clean slate at birth, ready to be scribbled on.' The more he talked, the more mesmerized she became. She suspected that he preferred her not to rise to the intellectual occasion and so she complied. She was content just to bathe in his genius.

He had a complicated private life as well. He'd been divorced twice but was always vague on the details of how his marriages had ended. Arabella intuited that he had been badly hurt; this was his only scissure of vulnerability and she cherished it. In the end it was the combination of his perfect mind and fractured heart that purged her own misgivings about love.

He told her she was beautiful in a manner that was genuine and not the least bit threatening. He made her feel *so* beautiful she began to get the occasional twinge of pride. One day in the spring of 1976, she wore a blouse with the top button undone. It showed off her cleavage. Eric told her she was divine.

Divine.

She sang the word to herself all day and bought a snug-fitting sweater the next.

One night in winter he took her figure skating on Beaver Lake. It was a cold clear night with a purple sky. When they spoke to each other, their words came out mingled with cloudy puffs of their frozen breath. Eric was a good skater and was showing off. He hurled his gangly frame into the air and spun around twice, arms and legs askew, before landing on the ice with a flump.

'That was a double lutz,' he told her.

She helped him up.

As they skated off towards the chalet he was hobbling slightly from the pain in his coccyx.

'Once,' he wheezed, 'I could stick the landings.'

Inside the chalet, they shared a watery hot-chocolate in a paper cup. Ara scalded her tongue but savoured the pain of the burn; it was sharp and uncomfortable, and she knew later on it would help her senses to remember that night.

They were sitting side by side on a wooden bench by the lockers. 'My feet hurt,' she said.

'Here,' he offered. 'Let me help you.'

He knelt down in front of her and untied her laces. One after the other, he eased her stockinged feet from the skates and began to massage them tenderly. Her toes were bent and squashed, numb from the tight skates. He handled each foot tentatively, as though it were a hamster. Then he looked up into her dreamy face and said, 'Will you marry me?'

Her breath caught and she accidentally bit down on her already throbbing tongue. It was like a jolt of electricity. This delighted her. Now she would forever associate her love for him with a raw, sore tongue.

'Yes,' she answered, delirious. 'Yes, yes, yes!'

He kissed her gnarled toes to seal the deal.

They were married by her twenty-second birthday, the year of her college graduation. On their honeymoon in Puerto Vallarta, she bled through the white cotton sheet. Eric was thrilled. The blood made her think of rose petals.

The petals dried up quickly. Arabella got pregnant, had a baby girl, and watched her magnificent breasts stretch and fall. Eric screwed her night and day, even when she was sore and exhausted. Afterwards he went out and got drunk in the student bars around campus. He no longer found her divine. And when their daughter was three, when he'd used up Arabella's body until it no longer held any mysteries for him, he left her for a nineteen-year-old economics major with gold hair.

Eric paid alimony and child support for little Dayna, albeit irregularly, right up until Arabella married Roman Boot two years later.

She met Roman at the hospital when she sprained her ankle tripping over Dayna's Malibu Barbie beach house. He was the attending X-ray technician and he fell for her right away. He pursued her until she relented.

What he is, and what he probably was all along, is a last-resort sort. She blames her unhappiness on her mother's doomsday attitude because she hadn't been looking for romance when she stumbled into the hospital to get her swollen ankle X-rayed. It was Melva who urged her to go out with Roman.

'It's your last chance,' Melva had warned ominously. 'You've got a kid now and you've put on some weight in your bee-hind. If that X-ray technician wants a date with you, you should count yourself lucky and accept.'

Arabella had no reserves of better judgement to fall back on; it went back to her childhood, to growing up without a solid foundation. Maybe it had to do with her real father getting blown up, or Cyrus spying on her, or Melva's peculiar and at times questionable method of parenting. Whatever the reason, Arabella wasn't so much a potential partner for Roman as she was his prey. During their courtship, the words *it's your last chance* must have been beating like bongo drums in her subconscious because she fell for him like a pigeon shot out of the sky.

It was a glorious courtship, highlighted by rollerskating, mini-golf expeditions, long drives up North and Roman's exquisite adoration for her.

At his insistence, they were married in the X-ray room at the hospital. He loved his job that much. She admired his devotion and felt it boded well for their future.

Who but a psychic could have predicted that marriage would transform him into the selfish couch-potato he became only months after they exchanged I-dos?

Granted, he isn't abusive or complex like Eric was. And as husbands go he makes an adequate living, he has a youthful athletic physique and he never complained that she already had a child, which some men might have objected to.

She went into the marriage wearing optimistic sunglasses. She never wanted to be one of those divorcées who get hitched again because their ex-husband's alimony cheques are getting more and more sporadic and the kid needs corrective shoes. She didn't want to marry again only because she missed going to movies on Cheap Tuesday and chatting with someone older than four years old at the breakfast table. She wanted it to last. She wanted to marry a second time for love.

A MAGNIFICENT BODY

* * *

On their first date they went rollerskating at Caesar's Palace. Roman was a whiz on wheels. He dominated the rink with prowess and confidence, dragging a wobbly Ara behind him as though she were a cumbersome trailer. But he was patient and generous. He taught her how to use the rubber stopper on her skate so she wouldn't have to keep crashing into the sideboards. He bought her a tub of neon-yellow popcorn and tucked his hand into the back pocket of her jeans while they skated to the slow songs. When 'Funky Town' thundered down from the speakers, he got as excited as a kid at the zoo. 'I love this song!' he cried, and took off, skating away energetically to the beat.

'This is our song!' he once called out to her, as he floated past in a roller-frenzy. 'Okay?'

She nodded, charmed by his enthusiasm. His exuberance was medicinal. It was just what Ara needed at that stage of her life. And his papaya-shaped bum in snug Jordache jeans was awfully cute as he disco-glided round and round the rink.

Men and Steak

TANYA P. is Arabella's dearest friend. They met at Weight Watchers in 1987; their diets both failed, but the friendship survived. Tanya has a good heart buried somewhere beneath all the excess flesh. She tends to be gossipy and bossy and catty and bitter, but Arabella understands that the source of Tanya's hostile veneer is loneliness. Her obesity has made her sour, paralysingly envious of those more physically blessed than she. She only tolerates Ara because Ara has such a big bum.

'So he offered me a day at a spa,' Arabella announces.

'For your birthday?'

'Mmm. I just don't know how he would have thought of it. He's usually not in tune with my taste.'

'Maybe he asked your mother,' Tanya says off-handedly, plunging her spoon into a soft peak of chocolate mousse.

'Maybe.'

'The place will be crawling with anorexic Greene Avenue types,' Tanya warns.

Ara shrugs, checks her Swatch. 'I better get going,' she says. 'We're having steak tonight.'

'Ooooo, steak night. God forbid King Roman should go a night without beef.'

'You know how it is with men and steak. It's some kind of bond.'

'Like men and fishing,' Tanya says.

'Men and football.'

'Men and tools.'

'Roman's only bond with tools is that he *is* one,' Ara mutters.

'Ah, don't be so ungrateful. He got you a spa.'

'Hmm.'

What Arabella has learned about her husband, aside from the fact that he is homophobic and allergic to shellfish, is that his gestures of generosity are always tainted by ulterior motives. For instance, on their second wedding anniversary he bought her a Betamax. He gave her the enormous box in a great ceremonious gesture and said, 'Surprise!'

She tore it open and squealed with delight. It was the early eighties when VCRs were still a novelty. 'Oh, Roman,' she exclaimed. 'Now we can rent videos!' She was truly amazed by his generosity.

That's when he handed her another package, diligently wrapped and tied with ribbons. 'I'm one step ahead of you,' he said, winking. Beneath the pretty wrapping there were two videos: *Annie Hole* and *Kramer Does Kramer*. It took all the joy out of the Betamax for Ara. She understood then that her gift was really *his* gift to himself.

'The spa makes me nervous,' Ara confides to Tanya. 'Roman's gifts usually cost me the high price of self-respect.'

Later on, in her kitchen, Ara drops three butter buds into a frying pan, ever conscious of Roman's cholesterol level. She watches it bubble and sizzle, then lays two steaks in it.

'Cook it till it's well done this time!' Roman screams from the bathroom. 'Last time it was raw in the centre!'

Roman always locks himself in the bathroom before dinner. He likes to clear his bowels before he eats so there's more room for the food.

In a separate pan, Ara stir-fries a handful of chopped tofu, snow peas and broccoli for Kenny. He's only twelve but staunchly committed to life as a vegetarian – has been ever since he was six years old and the four of them were out for dinner at a French restaurant, Le Lapin Farci. After reading the menu, little Kenny looked up, horrified, and said, 'Look, Mommy, they serve bunnies here!'

'Lots of people eat rabbit, son.'

He began to cry.

'What do you think you're eating when you have bacon or steak or a cheeseburger at McDonald's?' Roman said heartlessly.

The boy was confused. He looked over at his mother, then at his sister who was giggling.

'Hamburgers come from chopped-up cows,' Dayna taunted.

'And bacon is nothing but a slaughtered pig, son.'

Kenny ran to the fancy bathroom and vomited. He never ate meat or poultry again, an admirable gesture but a colossal pain in the neck for Ara, who has to cook him a special supper every night.

When the steaks are done and the potatoes baked, she calls Roman and Kenny into the kitchen. The household is a lot more harmonious with Dayna away at college. As Dayna marched confidently through her teenage years, her tolerance for Roman flatlined. Now she can barely acknowledge him with civility. She calls him the Boob and thinks he's stupid compared to her real father, the professor (although Eric wants nothing to do with her, so there you have it.)

In the end though, what went fundamentally wrong in the Boot household was not Dayna's fault at all but rather a noticeable lack of parental bonding on Roman's end. There is a gaping void where there should be a father. Roman is more like a tenant renting space in the house. He's around enough, on the couch watching TV or reading Penthouse in the bathroom. Occasionally he takes Kenny to the Mini-Putt, a sport at which he himself excels. But right from the beginning it was as if the children were stray pets he'd taken in as a noble gesture – two hungry cats who owed him big, but who could never win his love.

Ara can understand the strained relationship between Roman and her daughter. Step-relationships are notoriously complicated and not always successful. But Roman shows the same indifference towards Kenny, his own son, his flesh and blood.

Ara has done her best to compensate for Roman's shortcomings, to bring sufficient doses of happiness to her children's lives. She has made sure to build their egos and replenish any self-esteem which may have leaked out due to reasons beyond her control. She has provided for them what she herself was denied. She's done a good job too and, on certain days, she might even find herself quite satisfied with her life. Anyhow, she is not one for futile and self-indulgent bouts of self-pity or introspection.

Meanwhile, life on the home front is a good deal calmer without Dayna, but Ara still misses her daughter's bubbly spirit and Hollywood gossip. Dayna is studying to be a journalist at a college in New York, the very city where her flesh-and-blood grandfather was blown up. Ara had reservations at first, but Dayna got a scholarship and wasn't letting *anyone* stand in her way. She wants to work for a tabloid eventually – the *National Enquirer* or the *Globe*. She dreams of someday having her own show on TV – *Talk Trash* – for the dirt on Hollywood's finest. The girl is an encyclopaedia of information on the lives of the rich and famous. Ara worries that her daughter's grasp on reality is slipping, but her grades at college indicate the opposite.

'Do we have HP sauce?' Roman wants to know.

Ara grabs the narrow bottle from the fridge. 'Here,' she says, motioning for him to carry it to the table himself. Roman settles into his seat at the head of the table and waits for his steak to arrive. Kenny saunters in next and pulls out his chair without looking at his father. Ara carries the food to the table and sits down opposite Roman.

Kenny eyes the stir-fry unexcitedly. 'This is the twelfth stir-fry you've made me this month,' he comments. 'And it's only the 23rd.'

'My vegetarian repertoire is limited,' Ara snaps.

'What about the cookbook I bought you for Christmas?' Kenny complains. 'There were hundreds of recipes in there.'

'I don't have all day to cook for the both of you, you know.'

Kenny sulkily jabs his fork into a lump of tofu. 'You could at least vary the vegetables.'

'Why don't you stop complaining and eat a damn steak?' Roman barks.

'I don't eat animals, Dad.'

Roman picks up his steak with his bare fingers and dangles it in front of Kenny's face. 'This is no animal, son. This is a delicious slab of meat.'

'But it *was* a cow,' Kenny retorts, squirming away from the steak.

'Big deal. What are cows good for otherwise? Besides, once the steak is cooked it's no longer considered an animal.'

'Not true!'

Roman sighs. 'It's just not right,' he says, limply dropping the steak back onto his plate. 'A boy who doesn't eat meat.'

'Leave him alone,' Ara says.

'I've never heard of a boy not liking steak! The bone, the blood, the juicy and succulent meat, the crisp fat …'

Kenny blocks his ears defiantly.

'Maybe he's queer,' Roman says pensively.

* * *

That night Roman is determined to prove his manhood – most likely a counter-attack against having fathered a son who doesn't eat meat. Before coming to bed he rinses his mouth with Listermint, then dabs some on his neck and wrists. He opens the top button of his beige two-piece pyjama shirt and smooths the tangled hairs on his chest. Emerging from the bathroom into the bedroom, he says seductively, 'Let's get it on.'

Ara is curled on her side with her back to him. 'I'm sleepy,' she mutters.

Roman leaps onto the bed in belly-flop style, landing prostrate beside her. 'Mr Big is ready for action,' he says.

Ara rolls her eyes. 'Tell him I have a headache.'

Roman presses his hard-on into her lower back. 'Mr Big won't take no for an answer,' he says, then licks her ear lobe. 'Get naked, babe.'

Ara swats his face. 'Go away,' she says impatiently.

'Arabella, we haven't done it since early June,' he whines. 'We're nearing the four-month mark.'

She shrugs.

Undaunted, he puts his hand on her shoulder and tries to pull her towards him. She tenses her muscles so tight her body is stiffer than rigor mortis.

'Come on,' he begs.

She feigns a light snore. Roman pants into the back of her head for a few more minutes and then gives up, rolling over to the other side of the bed. 'A lot of women would *pay* for a go at Mr Big,' he sulks. 'A lot of women would pay.'

Le Spa

ARA PAUSES OUTSIDE the elegant front doors of Le Spa. She thinks about the hordes of rich, muscle-toned women lurking inside and wishes, not for the first time, that she'd appreciated the magnificent body of her youth while she still had it. Now it's her butt she hides under baggy sweaters.

She takes a breath and throws open the doors, preferring to make a grand entrance rather than the meek, apologetic sort she might once have made. She is forty, after all.

The floors and front desk are off-white marble with beige veins. There is a fountain smack in the centre of the lobby, splashing water onto anyone who gets close. The ceilings are high with beams of red, yellow and green light streaming through a stained-glass skylight.

'Yoohoo.'

Ara turns around so she is facing the front desk. The man sitting behind it is waving his delicate white hand. Pale, wispy and proudly effeminate, he has the look of a Mummenshanz mime in his black turtleneck and black pants. He wears a gold hoop in either ear and a pencil-thin moustache above his lip. There is a small pink triangle pinned to his chest. He is immaculately coiffed and smells of hair salon shampoo. 'Can I help you?'

'I have a gift certificate.'

'Lovely,' he says, waiting for her to draw it from her purse. He frowns as she hands it to him. 'The Bare Essentials Package?' he remarks.

'Pardon?'

'Your gift certificate is for the Bare Essentials Package.'

'Is there a problem?'

He smiles in that way Parisians smile at American tourists – an even mix of loathing and superiority. 'Of course not, Madame Boot. Please, have a seat in the lounge and Vula will be with you in a moment.'

Ara plunks herself onto one of four taupe suede couches in the lounge and picks up an *US* magazine with Meg Ryan on the cover. Meg's hair is cut in an adorable pixie style with light blond wisps at the front. Ara wonders if she could carry off such a hair style. Maybe she'll ask the coiffeuse today.

She flips through the magazine, stopping to read the 'Faces & Places' section which Dayna got her hooked on years ago. Now, looking at pictures of Michael Jackson and Oprah Winfrey, she thinks about her daughter in New York City and she wonders if one day she'll see Dayna's name in print – *Dayna Slominski, Editor* on the masthead of *US* magazine. Wow, she muses indulgently, that would be something.

'Ms Boot? I'm Vula, your hostess.' Vula holds out a well-manicured hand. Her skin is smooth and translucent, her handshake confident. She slides onto the taupe suede couch beside Ara. 'Let's take care of some business first.' She scribbles something onto her clipboard and then says, 'I see you've chosen the Bare Essentials Package.'

'It was a gift.'

Vula nods curtly. 'Well, if that's what you got …'

'What else is there?'

'Our mid-range option is the Princess-for-a-Day. But our most popular package is the Belle-of-the-Ball. It's a no-holds-barred beauty extravaganza.'

'What do I get with the Bare Essentials?'

Vula's lips curl into a sneer. 'You're entitled to two treatments and two activities. You can choose from the pool, the fitness centre, a fitness evaluation, the sauna, and the snack bar – eating is considered an activity. In the treatment category, you're entitled to a manicure, a hair cut and a leg/moustache wax. You do *not* have access to a massage, a facial, a make-over, a mud bath, a pedicure, meditation, tai chi, tae kwan do, step class, aerobics, the hot tub, or the bistro.'

'Couldn't you make an exception and sneak me into a mud bath?' Ara asks. 'It's my fortieth birthday.'

Vula shakes her head with a flagrantly insincere smile. 'I can't make exceptions, Ms Boot. We have a system.'

'My husband might not have known –'

'We have a system,' she snaps. 'Perhaps you'd like to pay the difference for the Belle-of-the-Ball.'

'But it's *my* birthday. I'm not paying for my own gift.'

'Then you should take that up with your husband, Ms Boot. We have –'

'Yes, I know – *a system.*' Ara would like to shove that system right up Vula's aerobicized ass. She'd also like to clobber Roman on that block of wood he calls a head.

'Have you decided how you'd like to spend the day?' Vula presses, casting her eyes down at her watch. 'Might I suggest a fitness evaluation?'

Ara trembles with a combination of fury and humiliation but in a noble effort to salvage the day, she ponders her options calmly. She chooses: the pool, haircut, manicure and snack bar. Vula says, 'Sergei will check your bag and give you a robe,' and then click-clicks across the marble floor in her pine-coloured pumps.

The day begins at the swimming pool. Ara, wrapped in a thick warm towel with Le Spa monogrammed above her left breast, sits on the ledge of the pool and dips her feet. She fiddles with the badge around her neck, which itemizes the activities and treatments she is entitled to. The smell of chlorine drifts up to her nostrils, reminds her of the YMCA day camp where Dayna had swimming lessons every Tuesday for five years.

'LET'S MOVE IT!!'

Startled, Ara jerks her head up in search of a face to match the shrill voice. She immediately spots a muscular woman, solid as a stump and wearing a black Speedo bathing suit, ploughing towards her at full speed. 'You have two options here,' the woman bellows. 'Laps or water aerobics. You're not here to sit around on your rear end all day. Are you?'

'I wouldn't mind relaxing –'

'Well, *I* mind. Now hep hep. Into the water. Get moving.'

So Ara leaves the safety of her fluffy Le Spa towel and eases herself into the water. 'Laps or water aerobics,' the stocky Speedo woman says again. 'Choose your section of the pool.'

Ara backstrokes leisurely for twenty minutes up and down the length of the pool. She closes her eyes and thinks about Roman, the way he had the choice between the Belle-of-the-Ball and Bare Essentials and chose the cheaper one. Maybe she's ungrateful – he *did* choose the spa himself – but there's a nagging rage bubbling under her surface. He could have picked Princess-for-a-Day. Isn't she at least worth the mid-range price? She swallows a gulp of chlorinated water, which squirts out her nose and burns her throat. She starts to choke. Gasping for breath with each doggy paddle, she lunges for the ledge with flailing arms.

'I don't know whether to help you or let you drown,' he says.

Ara, purple-faced and coughing up water, recognizes the voice. She has heard it over and over again in her nightmares. She looks up apprehensively into the smug face of her ex-husband. 'Eric …' she stammers.

He thrusts his arm out to her and tugs her out of the pool. 'Thanks,' she mutters reluctantly. 'I got water in my mouth.'

'It *is* a pool.'

'Ha ha,' she snorts, assessing the way his physique has drooped and sagged over the years. He's always had that jellyfish posture so it's difficult for her to gauge the extent to which he has been ravaged by age. She is pleased to note he is sporting a gold toupee that resembles an empty bird's nest. Otherwise he is essentially the same man who once vowed to love and cherish her until death did them part. 'What are you doing here?' she asks, placing her hands on her hips in stand-off position. 'Did you come for a gratuitous mouth-to-mouth resuscitation from the seventeen-year-old lifeguard?'

'I've missed your acerbic wit,' he says.

'It's missed you.'

'You've put on weight,' he remarks.

'And your hair looks like it was built by a family of robins.'

'This hair piece is a Maurice Poupée.'

'Did it come with birds?'

'This from a woman whose body weight makes it impossible for her to stay afloat in the water. You're in no position to launch insults, Babar.'

Ara stares longingly at the robe, which is crumpled in a heap at the opposite end of the pool. How she would love to cover herself up and hide from Eric's scrutinizing stare. Those grey eyes of his are like two unforgiving magnifying glasses, blowing all her flaws into grotesque proportions.

'How's Dayna?' he asks, folding his arms across his bony white chest. His nipples are brown, shriveled like rotting grapes. Ara looks away.

'Try asking her yourself,' she snaps. 'You could phone her once in a while, you know.'

'It's long distance.'

'She's your daughter.'

'I do my best.'

'Your best sucks.'

'Give her my regards. And Aurora sends kisses.'

'Aurora? Which one is Aurora? Number six or seven?'

'We can't all be as happy as you and the Boob,' he quips, unable to resist a self-satisfied smile.

'The Boob and I are *very* happy,' she fires.

'Well, this has been a delightful reunion,' he says. 'Nay, it's been enlightening. But I'm off to join Aurora for tai chi and a full body massage.'

Ara blinks back tears. 'You paid for the Belle-of-the-Ball package?' she asks him.

'Of course.'

'For Aurora?'

'Indeed.' Then he notices her day pass, with the words BARE ESSENTIALS printed in block letters. The humiliation is unbearable. He chuckles, then waves a deprecating little wave. 'Ta-ta,' he says.

Ara watches him disappear into the men's locker room with something like a paperweight pressing on her chest. Her day is in shambles and so is her spirit.

Happy birthday.

There is something about bumping into an ex-husband which triggers a surge of hunger, or at least the urge to binge. With her hair wrapped turban-style on top of her head, Ara heads for the snack bar at the back of the lobby, which is nothing but a counter skimpily lined with health food – bananas, yogurt, Evian, non-fat date squares, and the Rice Cake Platter consisting of two rice cakes, a sliver of goat cheese and a couple of slices of cucumber.

Starving, Ara orders the date square and a cup of tea, which do little to satisfy her hunger or silence the rumbling in her stomach. She is preoccupied with a recurring vision of Eric and his wife enjoying a massage; of Aurora Slominski being treated like a Belle (whatever *that* is) while Ara pitifully nibbles on a date square. Hating Roman with an awakening passion, she fantasizes about having the words *Bare Essentials* tattooed across his forehead, because that's all he is in the husband department.

After a skimpy lunch even a model would deem an appetizer, Ara makes her way upstairs to the hair salon. She passes Le Bistro and scans the menu bitterly, salivating: *Pasta Primavera with fresh spring vegetables and sprigs of homegrown parsley. Grilled salmon with lemon-garlic dressing and Mexican rice. Chef's salad with slices of smoked turkey and cubelets of feta cheese.* Ara considers hiding her day pass deep inside her cleavage and sneaking inside but not long after the break-up with Eric she vowed to stop using her breasts for personal gain.

For a split second she contemplates spying on Eric and Aurora in the tai chi room. But what if Aurora has a marvelous figure? It's an avenue better left unexplored. So far the day's string of events has effectively sliced chunks off Ara's self-esteem like big pieces of cake. Spying on her ex-husband and his younger bride would inevitably leave her with just a few crumbs.

At the salon, she gladly sinks into a comfortable swivel chair, her freshly washed hair wrapped in another monogrammed towel. She sits facing herself in the mirror. She notices a new line or two around her mouth.

'I'm Leslie, your manicurist.'

'And I'm Sela, your hairdresser.'

Ara looks up. 'I'm getting the cut and manicure at the same time?' she says limply.

They nod in unison, smiling like the Beautician-Bobbsey twins. 'It's more cost-efficient.'

'Of course.'

Leslie delicately takes Ara's hands in her own and absently begins to buff them. Sela says, 'What can I do for you?'

'I was thinking of something like Meg Ryan's new hair do.'

Sela smiles sympathetically. 'Isn't that a little too cutesy? I mean it's all right on Meg, but ...'

'Then whatever you think is best.'

Sela gets to work snipping at Ara's head with mild enthusiasm.

'By the way, I know who Frank is sleeping with,' Leslie announces, dragging the emery board across Ara's nails.

'Who?'

'I can deal with the cheating, you know? I mean, *honestly*, can we really expect any man to be monotonous?'

'Monogamous,' Ara corrects.

'Whatever. But it's *her*.'

'What about her?' Sela asks, as chunks of Ara's dirty blond hair slide down her plastic cape and land in her lap. 'Is something wrong with her?'

Leslie heaves a dramatic sigh, then blows on Ara's fingers. 'It's so embarrassing,' she whispers.

'What is it?' Sela gasps. 'Does she bleach?'

'Worse.'

'She's fat?'

'It's not that bad. *That* would be the ultimate embarrassment.'

'What then?'

Leslie snatches a tissue from a floral box on her nail polish cart, dabs at the corner of her eyes and whispers, 'She has a mono-brow.'

The Ultimate Embarrassment

ARA SLAMS HER CAR DOOR, stomps up the front walk to her house and shoves her key into the lock. She is surprised to find the door open but it's not the first time she's forgotten to lock it in the morning. Roman is always barking at her for being so absent-minded. 'I have valuable possessions in this house,' he says. He is referring to a sound system he bought in 1978 with a turntable and eight-track tape player, a twelve-inch TV that doesn't even work with a remote control, and a vintage collection of Penthouse magazines.

Ara hangs her keys on the key hook she installed herself to keep her from misplacing them time after time. She heads straight for the kitchen, straight for the freezer, straight for the Häagen Dazs. She drops into a chair at her kitchen table and plunges her spoon into the ice cream. She has a preference for chocolate-chocolate chip but Kenny's skin reacts badly to cocoa so she buys French vanilla instead. These are the sacrifices a mother has to make.

After feeding herself, Ara feeds Kenny's fish, Gefilte. As she's shaking fish food into the tank, she hears what sounds from a distance like a growling dog. She replaces the fish food on the shelf and listens carefully. The noise is coming from upstairs. 'Hello?' she calls out nervously, moving closer to the bottom of the staircase. The growling gets louder, gruffer. There is the occasional bark too and as Ara climbs the stairs cautiously and ever so quietly, she is almost positive the dog is in her bedroom. She tiptoes down the carpeted hall and pauses outside the door. The barking gets louder and more frenzied, and then suddenly comes to stop. The house falls silent.

Ara throws open the door. There on the floor, naked but for a silver spiked dog collar around his neck, is Roman. Beside him lies Tanya, just as naked, with her round peaceful face pressed into his armpit.

'I'm home from the spa,' Ara announces.

Roman jostles for something to throw over Mr Big, who is quickly becoming Mr Tiny.

'Surprise,' Ara says flatly.

Roman shoves Tanya out of his armpit. He is looking up at Ara pitifully, tugging on the dog collar with one hand and shielding his penis with the other. 'A-Ara –' he sputters lamely. 'It's not what you think.'

Ara's head throbs. She feels blurry, dazed. Shame and anger heat up her face.

'This must seem very suspicious,' Roman continues, wiping beads of sweat from his forehead. 'Very suspicious indeed.'

Tanya snatches a sheet off the bed to cover herself. Her fat cheeks are the colour of plums. 'How was the spa?' she asks Ara, her tone deliberately casual. 'Did you get a facial? You look rosy.'

'Rosy?'

'We didn't expect you back so soon,' she says.

'I gather the spa was your idea,' Ara spits.

'Did you think *he* thought of it?' Tanya chortles, pointing at Roman. He is standing up now, blank and silent like the object of a show-and-tell presentation. 'Roman wanted to send you snowshoeing! *Of course* the spa was my idea.'

Ara snatches up the crystal vase Eric gave her long ago and launches it across the room at a blank patch of the wall. It smashes to pieces, the shards of glass sprinkling all over the carpet. 'How could you do this to me?' she bellows.

'It was a mistake,' Roman whines. 'You weren't supposed to find out.'

'You aren't supposed to be back yet,' Tanya throws in.

'Well, Marmaduke here is so cheap he bought me the Bare Essentials Package instead of the Belle-of-the-Ball,' Ara explains. 'It took all of one hour and forty-five minutes. I didn't even get a pedicure.'

Tanya shoots a *you moron* look over at Roman. He tugs nervously at the dog collar again, which is starting to chafe and leave a rash. 'I'm sorry, Cottonball,' he murmurs, dropping onto the edge of the bed. His head slumps into his chest and he makes a rather lame attempt at covering his limp penis with his hand. 'But Ara,' he adds, 'you're not entirely blameless.'

'I beg your pardon?'

'I'm a man!' he proclaims. 'And I need regular sexual release. You wouldn't allow me to drink of your milk, so I had to find another cow!' He looks over at Tanya. 'Or whatever,' he says.

Ara heaves a weighty sigh filled with too many past disappointments and a future that promises little more. Roman and Tanya are staring at her.

'What is it?' she snaps.

'Your hair,' Roman says. 'What happened to your hair?'

Ara's hand instinctively goes to her head. Sela gave her an old person's hair-do – short and puffy, brushed over the ears and hairsprayed for maximum height. No white-blond wisps like Meg Ryan, that's for sure. 'Sela thought I needed a more mature look now that I'm forty.'

'I'm not crazy about all that height,' Tanya remarks. 'Big hair is out.'

'She's right,' Roman agrees.

'Is this the first time?' Arabella asks Tanya.

'It *would* have been,' Tanya mumbles. 'We've been planning for weeks ...'

Ara turns to Roman, her ego shattered in as many pieces as the vase. The vase, at least, can be replaced. 'Why?' she says in a small voice. 'Why, Roman?'

'Mr Beef was lonely,' Roman confesses humbly. 'That's all. He was just lonely.'

Ara shakes her head, burdened as much by the inconvenience of it all as by the predictable feelings of anger and jealousy. Although Roman is bland as a tuna fish sandwich, she is wounded by the sudden blast of infidelity. Roman's flaws do little to cushion the blow of rejection.

'I'll have to leave,' she says calmly.

'Don't go,' Roman pleads. 'We can work through this.'

Ara eyes him wearily in all his nude, doggy-collared splendour. 'I've never been a dog lover,' she says.

'Spare us the dog jokes,' Tanya mutters.

'They're all I have left. Now both of you leave the room so I can pack my things.'

She looks around her then, trying to decide where to begin. The closet? The dresser? The file boxes of photographs and letters she keeps under her bed? She notices Roman and Tanya still staring at her. 'Go away,' she seethes, all the quiet rage of the last few years crystallizing into rock-hard strength.

Roman sighs, pulling on a pair of boxers – the ones with *Nice Ass!* printed on the back.

Ara says, 'At least you didn't ruin my chintz bedspread.'

'I'm sorry, Cottonball.' He shuffles out of the bedroom with Tanya padding behind him wrapped toga-style in the sheet. Near the door Tanya whispers, 'Why didn't you just splurge and make her a Belle?'

Loud enough so Arabella can hear, Roman answers, 'The Bare Essentials Package came with a free pair of flip-flops.'

Alone in her room, Ara sits down on the bed and weeps. Imagine, a man like Roman cheating on *her*. Betrayal gurgles in her chest like indigestion. His shortcomings are irrelevant; they just make the episode all the more degrading. Now she goes across the room and kneels down on all fours to pick up the broken pieces of the crystal vase. She doesn't want anyone to cut their feet.

Later, Ara struggles down the stairs dragging two suitcases – one for her and one for Kenny. She doesn't want to take much. Her life with Roman is not one she necessarily wants to remember or cherish. Besides, there is little of sentimental value worth salvaging.

She finds Tanya and Roman sitting in the kitchen, facing each other miserably at the table, their bedroom escapade now nothing but an embarrassing fiasco. Funny how passion can spoil so fast, like a cut-open avocado.

'I'm off,' Ara says.

'Where are you going?'

'First to pick Kenny up from school.'

'And then?'

Ara shrugs. 'I'll let you know.'

'What about my son?'

'You never cared for him much anyway.'

'He's still my son.'

'You'll hear from us,' she says, looking at Tanya critically.

She carries her two suitcases to the vestibule. Roman and Tanya trail after her awkwardly. Ara stops at the door and turns to face them. 'You know,' she says, pulling the door open triumphantly, 'I feel quite liberated.'

'Will you be back?'

'Who knows? But I'm taking the car.' She knows Roman is in no position to argue. His expression is stolid, blank except for a twitch in his left eye. A twitch of guilt or regret over losing his car? She'll never know. She doesn't much care.

Ara trots down her three front steps. She feels light. She has never felt so light. 'Enjoy him,' she says to Tanya. And it's as though the paperweight on her chest is gone.

Louisiana Way

'WHERE ARE WE GOING?'

'Grandma's,' she says, screeching out of the parking lot.

'Why are you picking me up from school now? It's not even three-thirty.'

'So we can beat the traffic on the Champlain Bridge.'

'Why are you speeding? You're going eighty in a fifty-kilometre zone.'

'You're right,' she says, easing up on the gas. 'Speed kills.'

'Do we have a map?' Kenny says, rifling through the glove compartment.

'I know the way. I used to visit Grandma every year when I was in college.'

'How long does it take to get there?' Kenny wants to know. He has only met his grandmother twice, both times when they flew down for Christmas in the early eighties.

'Oh, three days or so,' Ara says.

'Three days? What about school? I have no clothes. What about my toothbrush?'

'I packed for you.'

'Did you bring my blue pyjamas?'

'And your brown ones.'

Kenny reaches over and lowers the volume on the radio. He turns to face his mother. 'I don't understand,' he says.

'What I'm doing might scar you for life, Kenny. They say a boy needs his father.'

'We left Dad?'

'I wanted to be queen for a day, Kenny.'

He stares back at her, perplexed.

'Plus he cheated on me with Tanya.'

'She's gross.'

'Mmm.'

'Did you say goodbye?' he asks.

'Sort of. I feel guilty for dragging you into it, taking you to a new city and all, so far away. I just hope you can forgive me.'

'I forgive you. Dad doesn't like me much anyway.'

'Oh, sure he does. He loves you.'

Kenny snorts. 'He thinks I'm queer.'

'He doesn't understand you.'

'Will I ever see him again?'

Ara thinks about it for a minute or two. Then she says, 'That'll be up to you. If and when you want to see him we'll put you on a bus back home for however long you want. I don't want you to end up hating me for depriving you of some semblance of a relationship with your father.'

'Did you pack my Game Boy?'

'It's in your suitcase.'

They stop at a McDonald's drive-thru for dinner – only because the pickin's are slim on the highway. Kenny eats a Filet-o-Fish and Ara has her usual quarter-pounder with double mustard only. Ara looks thoughtful as she chews on a mouthful of beef. 'It's funny, isn't it, the way a burger can taste exactly the same in Montreal *and* New York state, as though they were all cooked by the same chef?'

'I don't think you can call them *chefs*,' Kenny says.

'Whatever. You used to appreciate McDonald's when you were little. Remember eating Happy Meals with Dayna?'

'She always stole my fries.'

'Then I'd give you mine.'

'You're a good mother,' Kenny says, and it brings two lone tears to her eyes. Maybe they do notice the sacrifices, she thinks.

'Let's play the roadkill game!'

'Oh, it depresses me, Kenny. It's so morbid. And you being a vegetarian and all.'

'It passes the time.'

'Okay. Five points for squirrels and chipmunks. Ten for raccoons and rabbits. Twenty-five for deer. Two points if it's unidentifiable.'

'Raccoon!' Kenny exclaims, jabbing his finger against the window. 'I see a raccoon! I have ten points.'

'There's a squirrel. Five points for me.'

Kenny shrugs, looking unconvinced. He stares intently out the window until he spots the next bloody animal corpse. 'Oh, I see another squirrel! Fifteen!'

Ara sighs. She hates to lose.

They drive along in competitive silence, each careful to keep their eyes focused on the side of the road. Ara has a competitive streak which rears its ugly head from time to time. Usually she gives in to her children, lets them win at Scrabble and gin rummy, go fish and Monopoly. But sometimes she just likes to win. This is one of those times. Unfortunately for them and for those members of the animal kingdom who play near the highway, it's dangerous to play games while driving. Ara gets so caught up in her search for a dead deer or at least a plump raccoon, she doesn't see the sneaky skunk dart right out in front of her car.

'Moooom!' Kenny shrieks. 'The sk*uuunk*!!' But it's too late and her front tire hits the poor little guy and he comes flying out in front of the windshield and lands with a pathetic thud on the side of the road. The stench explodes in the air like chemical warfare. Ara frantically rolls up her window, swearing and muttering under her breath so as not to corrupt her son.

'How many points for hitting a skunk?' Kenny asks.

Ara glares at him, pinching her nose and waving her hand frantically in front of her face to push the smell away from her nostrils.

'I think it's good luck,' Kenny consoles her.

'Killing an animal is never good luck.'

The next morning, after a restful sleep at a Quality Inn in Coxsackie, New York, they get back on Interstate 87 heading south. 'The car still stinks,' Kenny says, rolling down his window.

'We'll have to stop and buy air freshener at the next gas station,' she says. 'For now just try to ignore it.'

'But it's making me nauseous.'

'It's an omen.'

'What's an omen?'

'It's a bad sign.'

'Like foreshadowing?'

'Yes, exactly like foreshadowing, son.'

Kenny smiles, pleased with himself. Like his mother before him, he spends many hours lying on his bed reading. His teachers call him precocious. Last year, his report card said he was an exemplary student with lofty aspirations. Not bad for grade five. Sometimes he has to ask his mother what a certain word means, but once she tells him he never forgets.

They bump along for a few hours, passing signs for this state and that state. After New York, the states whiz by – Maryland, Delaware, D.C. In Washington, Kenny begs for a look at the White House. Ara, not one to refuse her only son an educational experience, takes a minor detour onto Pennsylvania Avenue. 'Oh wow!' he cries, as they cruise past the front gates. 'Do you think the president's in there now?'

'Well, it's lunch time. Maybe he's just sitting down to a bowl of Kraft Dinner with his family.'

'Oh, Mom, presidents doesn't eat Kraft Dinner.'

'Everyone eats Kraft Dinner.'

Across from the White House, an old hippie wearing camouflage pants and a T-shirt that says *Legalize It* gives Kenny the peace sign. 'Legalize *what?*' Kenny wants to know.

Ara shrugs her shoulders. 'Who knows?' she answers. She figures that one day in Kenny's near – but hopefully not *too* near – future, he will figure out what marijuana is. No sense rushing *that* part of his education. 'He's probably a Vietnam vet,' she says.

'Wow. I've never seen one before.'

'He's just a man, son. Like your father.'

'Except madder maybe.'

They continue in silence along the Theodore Roosevelt Memorial Bridge, until they pass the Arlington Cemetery where Ara explains to Kenny all about the eternal flame, John F. Kennedy, his wife Jackie, and the glorious Camelot era. Kenny listens, fascinated, until he notices a hitchhiker standing in front the *Welcome to Virginia!* sign.

'Hey, Mom,' he says. 'There's a lady hitchhiking.'

Ara looks out the passenger window at the young woman standing off to the side of the highway with her thumb sticking in the air. She's wearing faded jeans and a navy cardigan – the kind Ara used to wear with her kilt in high school. The girl is thin, wears no make-up, has unremarkable features. Her posture is poor – probably from exhaustion. There's a small army knapsack flung over her left shoulder.

To Kenny's horror, Ara veers off the highway. 'What are you doing, Mom?'

'I'm picking her up.'

'But she's a hitchhiker, Mom! This is the nineties, not the sixties. You should *never* pick up hitchhikers.'

'That's only if they're men, sweetie.'

'What if she's a serial killer?'

'Oh, pshaw!' Ara swats her hand dismissively. 'She looks tired and hungry and just plain sickly. Poor thing can't be older than twenty-five. See what I'm doing, Kenny? I'm helping out another woman. A *sister*. We women have to stick together and help each other out. There's a war going on, you know.'

'Between who?'

'Between men and women, son. And this poor girl is a soldier in *my* platoon.'

'Whose platoon am I in?' he asks.

'You're in my platoon,' she says. 'Little boys are fair game.' Then she sticks her head out the window, smiles at the hitchhiker and says, 'Hop in, sister!'

A Nice Gal From Yazoo

'I AM SOO GRATEFUL for this, ma'am. What a relief to get picked up by a family instead of some beer-bellied creep – you know the type – all BO and wanderin' hands. Although it does sorta stink in here. What'd y'all do – get sprayed by a skunk? No mattuh. I have some perfume in my bag. It's fake Giorgio – the next best thing and a damn lot better than eau de skunk!' She spritzes fake Giorgio into the air, improving the smell in the car almost immediately. 'There, that's better, ain't it?'

'Much.'

'Anyhow, you're a lifesaver, ma'am.' The hitchhiker thrusts her hand into the front seat. 'Georgia-Rae Pekoe from Yazoo City, Mississippi. That's Pekoe, like the tea.'

'Yazoo City?'

'It's about forty miles North of Jackson. I'm not surprised you ain't heard of it. Especially bein' from Canada and all. I noticed your licence plate says Québec.' She pronounces it *Kwi-beck*. 'I have a real eye for spottin' cool plates. Prob'ly from so much hitchhikin'. I think it's so neat, people visitin' my part of America from real far away. You know, like from up in Canada or California. Anyway, it's no wonder you never heard of Yazoo City. It ain't nothin' but a li'l polka dot on a map.'

'Where are you headed?'

'Back to Yazoo City. Just get me as far from Virginia as possible!'

Kenny bounces forward in his seat. 'How come?'

Georgia-Rae sighs. 'Well,' she begins, 'now that's a whole 'nother story. See, I was in Washington, D.C. on account of it was my daddy's birthday yesterday and I thought I would honour him by payin' a visit to the Vietnam Memorial. Daddy died in Nam during the Tet Offensive of '68, just two months before I was born. I never knew him, but Mama made sure I grew up knowin' what a kind and loving man he was. So, for his forty-fifth birthday I decided to do somethin' real special. I travelled all the way up here from Yazoo City, hitchhikin' all the way. You wouldn't believe how many truck drivers think they can feel you up just 'cause they're givin' you a ride!'

'Feel you up?' Kenny says.

'Never mind, son,' Ara scolds.

'So anyway,' Georgia-Rae twitters, 'I came all the way up here just to lay a single rose under his name on the Vietnam Memorial Wall. Let me tell you, it was a very emotional moment in my life.'

'Did you get a rubbing of his name on paper? They do that, you know.'

'I didn't know that. Next time maybe. That is, *if* there's a next time. See, I've encountered nothin' but bad luck since I got here. Some guy tried to pick me up at the Memorial. Would you believe the nerve? I know I'm attractive an' all, but there I was, payin' my respects to my daddy in what was a very emotional moment, and this guy – old, but not bad-lookin', mind you – is tellin' me I smell delicious. So I said very politely, "I'm wearin' Giorgio perfume which is why I smell so delicious, but right now I am havin' a private moment with my daddy, who was killed in the Tet Offensive." Of course I didn't tell him it was *fake* Giorgio.'

'And what did he say?'

Georgia-Rae whips open her knapsack and snatches a tissue from a Handy-Pak. She blows her nose like a trumpet. 'He was very gentlemanly. He said, "I apologize for disruptin' your private moment with your deceased father. I just had to let you know that you smell delicious." Well, I am just a sucker for a guy with manners and I was simply blown away. I told him if he was willin' to wait, I would have a rum and Coke with him later.'

'Then what?'

'We had a rum and Coke and got to talkin'. To make what could be a very long story short, Gus – that was his name – offered me a ride back to Yazoo City, which suited me just perfect because it saved me a long and potentially dangerous journey back. Turns out Gus is a Vietnam vet himself, from Arkansas, which is right by Yazoo City. I was thinkin' it was just too good to be true, but heck, I wasn't about to look a gift in the horse's mouth, was I? So we left right then and there and I was happier than a Mississippi mud pie. And then it happened.' She blows her nose again.

'What?'

'We weren't in his truck more than five minutes. We were barely out of D.C., just crossin' over into Virginia and, well, you can guess, can't you?'

Kenny shakes his head.

'Gus leaned over, shoved his hand right up my shirt, squeezed my nipple and said, "We can go to a motel or we can do it right here in the back of my truck."'

'Do what?' Kenny gasps.

'It, son, *it*,' Ara says. Kenny stares back, blank as fresh paper.

'You know,' Georgia-Rae explains. 'The baloney-pony.'

'Huh?'

Ara sighs. She was saving the sex talk till his thirteenth birthday, but now there's no getting around it. 'Intercourse, Kenny. Sexual intercourse.'

Kenny's eyes bulge. 'He wanted to pork you right there in the back of his truck?'

Ara's face turns the colour of a pale fish. Georgia-Rae bobs her head up and down. 'Exactly,' she says. 'Now, I'm no prude – let's be honest and call a spade a spade. But I'm no slut neither and I certainly was not about to jump in the back and screw some old Vietnam vet!'

'Georgia-Rae, please watch your language in front of the boy.'

Georgia-Rae blushes. 'Sorry. I just don't know of any other way to describe it because it certainly would *not* have been no makin' love, now would it?'

'I suppose not.'

'But ya never can tell how these creeps are gonna react to being turned down. Some fellas are good-natured and they just shrug and give you a lift to wherever you're goin' anyway. Some guys throw ya right out of the moving vee-hicle in the middle of Butt-fuck, Nowhere. But the worst creeps, well, you can imagine what they do.'

Ara shivers.

'Anyhow Gus threw me out of the truck. Called me a cock-tease – sorry about my language but that's exactly what he said, I'm just quotin'. And then he drove off and left me stranded in Virginia of all places.'

'Oh dear,' Ara mutters. 'What a degrading episode.'

'Thank goodness you came along, ma'am.'

'At least you managed to lay the rose at the Memorial,' Ara says thoughtfully. 'I'm sure your father was watching over you.'

'I hope so.'

'How did your dad die?' Kenny wants to know. 'Was he blown up? Did he step on a booby trap?'

'He was hidin' in a tree on a reconnaissance patrol. He got shot and hung on a branch for all his platoon to see as a warnin'.'

'Oh dear,' Ara says. 'How tragic.'

'Mama says the Vietnam War is like a big zit on America's history.'

'Indeed.'

'It was a mistake, you know. Sendin' good ole American boys to fight for a bunch a' chinks.'

Ara winces. 'You shouldn't harbour such ill will towards the Asians,' she says, turning to face Kenny. 'The correct terminology is *Asians*, son, not Chinks. But I can understand your bitterness, Georgia-Rae, what with losing your father over there.'

'He was only twenty when he died. That's just a kid, ain't it? I'm twenty-seven now and I ain't done nothin' noble or brave in my whole life.'

Ara touches Kenny's knee affectionately. She can't imagine losing him in another eight years, can't imagine having to say goodbye to her baby boy. Ever. 'War is a terrible game,' she says.

'Mama never remarried, you know.'

'Did your father get a medal?' Kenny asks.

'Oh, sure. Lots. Postu – post –'

'Posthumously.'

'Right!' she exclaims, clapping her hands together. 'Now here I am blabbin' my face off and I don't know *nothin'* about y'all. Like where are y'all goin' and such? It's not every day you see Kwibeckers from Canada headin' south. I never met a Canadian before.'

'We're going to visit my mother in Louisiana,' Ara explains. 'She lives in Lafayette.'

'We left my father,' Kenny adds.

'Oh no,' Georgia-Rae says, applying a coat of chalky pink lipstick to her lips. 'Another broken family.'

'Is that true, Mom?' Kenny says, wide-eyed and mortified. 'Are we broken?'

Ara flaps her hand in the air as though swatting a bug away from her face. 'Of course we're not broken. Bruised maybe.'

'Divorce is bad,' Georgia-Rae says sadly. 'Whatever happened to honouring them sacred marriage vows anyhow? Why the hell is it called a "vow" if it ain't gonna be stuck to? I thought vows was s'posed to be forever.' She pauses, and then: 'Hey, you folks like Huey Lewis and the News?'

'I'm not familiar with them.'

'Would you mind if I put a tape in?'

'Go ahead.'

She pulls a beat-up cassette from her knapsack and hands it to Kenny. He obediently pops it into the tape deck.

'They say a boy needs his father,' Georgia-Rae remarks. 'I don't mean to question your judgement, Miss Ara, but I know what it's like to grow up without a daddy.'

'So do I,' Ara says tightly, offended. 'And if you must know, I caught my husband in bed with my best friend.'

'Ouch. Been there.' She pats Kenny amicably on the back. And says, 'You'll be fine, kiddo.'

Kenny looks less sure and everyone settles into a pensive silence except Huey Lewis, who is crooning, 'I want a new drug.'

In the break between songs, Georgia-Rae leans forward with her arms folded on the back of Kenny's seat. She blows a fuchsia bubble with her Bubblicious. It pops with a loud snap. 'So your Mama lives in Lafayette,' she twitters. 'Have you ever tasted alligator-on-a-stick? We used to eat that whenever we visited New Orleans. Mmmm. You wouldn't think an alligator would have such flavour. You wouldn't even think an alligator was edible! But then I guess if we eat cows and chickies and piggies ...'

'I don't eat any of those animals,' Kenny says. 'I'm a vegetarian.'

'I guess you wouldn't eat alligator then.'

'I eat tuna fish and salmon in a can. I also eat clams and Filet-O-

Fish so I don't see why I wouldn't eat alligator. Fish aren't real animals.'

'Why not?' Georgia-Rae shrieks, offended. 'They swim and breathe and eat and go to school. Why ain't they real animals? I think that's unfair to fish, Kenny. It's downright hippo-critical.'

'In a way she's right,' Ara says. 'Why *do* you eat fish, son?'

Kenny shrugs. 'I didn't know fish were meat.'

'It's good protein, mind you. But if you're gonna stand up for somethin',' Georgia-Rae advises, 'then you better stand right up and not just halfway.'

They stop at Peg's 24-7 for grilled cheese sandwiches and coffee. Outside, a neon sign blinks Spec al – Babyback Ribs and ashed Pota oes. The menus are greasy and the lights are too bright, but there is nothing like the comforting ambiance of a diner on a long journey across the country. Ara and Georgia-Rae freshen up in the bathroom. They splash lukewarm water on their faces, wash their hands with pink liquid soap from the dispenser, and pee after carefully laying toilet paper on the seat.

Kenny is waiting for them in the booth when they get back. 'Can I play pinball, Mom? I ate all my sandwich.'

'What about your tomato soup?'

'It was cold. Besides, it tasted like ketchup.'

'All right. Here.' She hands him a dollar in quarters from a brown-and-beige pouch which she wears around her waist at all times. Inside the money belt she keeps what she calls her 'survival kit'. For years now she has been stashing and saving small change, chunks of Eric's alimony when it came, cash gifts from her stepfather and the odd bit of money Roman allotted her every now and again. After Eric left her out to dry, she vowed never to be left in a lurch again, never to wind up penniless and helpless in the face of another crumbled marriage.

'What do you do in Yazoo City?' Ara asks Georgia-Rae over hot black coffee.

'I work the meat counter at the Piggly Wiggly on South Main. Kenny sure would hate my job. All's I do is weigh and package raw meat – all slimy and bloody. Even I hate it sometimes. And you wouldn't believe what we do when nobody's lookin'. You could learn a thing or two from me. I could spare you gettin' salmonella poisoning, you know. You have to be a wise food shopper these days. I could change your opinion of grocery stores forever, ma'am.'

'I'm sure you could. Maybe I'd rather not know.'

'Okay, first off, you know them chickens with red paprika sprinkled all over 'em? Well the paprika means they've gone past their date. The more paprika, the older the bird. And do you know what my boss, Sal, does? He spits on dried-out rib eyes to make them look juicy. Now *that's* disgustin'. And that's only the beginnin'.'

'I think that's all I'd like to know.'

'They're worse in baked goods. They drop doughnuts and muffins an' shit, and then put them back to sell. My friend Dodie scoops icin' right off the chocolate cake with her finger and then sells it! The cake that is, not her finger. She'll be lickin' and pickin' at the cakes all day, spreadin' her saliva all over the icin' for some stranger to go home and eat at dessert. Yum yum, huh?'

'Mm.'

'It's the same everywhere, mind you, not just at the Piggly Wiggly on South Main. I don't wanna give my Piggly Wiggly a bad name because all supermarkets and bakeries do that shit, you know? There's nothin' else to do at work anyway. It's so dull sellin' food.' She pauses for a breath and then, more thoughtfully, 'Isn't it amazin' how even the most horrid cup of coffee tastes good at three o'clock in the mornin'?'

'I was just thinking the very same thing.'

'I bet you're one of them educated career gals, huh?'

Ara laughs. She has always been a housewife, preferring to stay home with Dayna and Kenny and watch them grow up at close range. She's fairly confident they appreciated her effort. 'I have a degree but no career,' she says.

'How come? What's the point of school if you ain't even gonna work?'

'I loved school. I studied philosophy. It's so pointless and vague. You can never really be wrong with philosophy and that made me feel better. I was very insecure.'

'You?'

'It's true,' Ara boasts. 'I used to be. Luckily my daughter is nothing like I was.'

'How old is she?'

'Eighteen. She just started her first year of college in New York.'

Georgia-Rae turns pale. 'Now *there's* a scary city. Bad things happen in that city, ma'am. You better tell your daughter to be careful.'

'She's got mace. Believe me, it wasn't my choice but she's so darn stubborn. She always makes up her own mind and then there's no arguing with her.' Ara sips her coffee, stirs a teaspoon of sugar into it, takes another sip. 'She's obsessed with fame.'

'She wants to be an actress?'

'No, she just wants to write about them.'

'Peculiar,' Georgia-Rae comments, dipping the tip of her doughnut into the coffee.

'You know, I was always afraid to have a daughter,' Ara says. 'I didn't want to raise a doormat or a victim. But Dayna's just the exact opposite – stubborn and strong and intimidating at times. Oh, she knows what she wants and no one is going to block her way. But it's Kenny I worry about. He's soft and maybe a little weird in some ways. He doesn't relate to the boys at his school. His own father doesn't much care for him either.'

'He's too smart,' Georgia-Rae says. 'People don't know what to make of smart boys 'cause there are so few of 'em in the world.'

Ara stares at Georgia-Rae and wonders how such precious pearls of wisdom can come from such a chalky pink mouth.

Around four o'clock in the morning they check into a motel off Highway 40. Ara collapses on her mattress without pulling down the bedspread or changing into her flannelette nightie. She doesn't even have the energy to tuck Kenny in the way she usually does. Instead she mutters 'goodnight' and leaves him alone with Georgia-Rae, who has graciously offered to sleep on the floor.

Kenny locks himself in the bathroom and washes his face. He doesn't brush his teeth because his breath smells okay and he didn't eat sweets all day. Besides, he isn't crazy over the taste of mint. He slips into his brown pyjamas and neatly folds his clothes. When he emerges, Georgia-Rae is sitting outside on the balcony. He joins her.

'What are you doing?' he asks her.

'I'm just lookin' out at the swimmin' pool.'

Kenny peers over the railing. The pool is covered in a blue plastic tarp and a lot of garbage.

'There's somethin' real depressin' about a swimmin' pool in the fall,' she says.

'I like fall because I hate wearing shorts in the summer.'

'Now why's that?'

'I have knobby knees,' Kenny says. 'My father says I have girl's legs.'

'Your legs'll grow up soon enough,' she assures him. 'I wouldn't worry about it.' She pulls a piece of tin foil from her jeans pocket and holds it under his nose.

'What's that?' he says.

'Can't you smell it? This is primo weed, Ken. Wanna get high?'

Kenny stares at her, trying not to betray his terror. 'I guess so,' he mutters.

Georgia-Rae smiles and rolls a joint. 'I pride myself on my ability to roll a perfect doobie. It's not everybody can boast such a skill. Most people can practise for years and never master it.' She lights her masterpiece and takes a long toke. 'Here,' she says, handing it to him. 'I suppose this is your first time.'

He nods.

'Just inhale, not too hard, then let it sink down into your lungs. Try not to cough it up, even if you have to.'

Kenny glances nervously at his mother, who is snoring peacefully on top of her bedspread. He puts the joint between his lips and draws a deep breath. The urge to cough is instantaneous but he remembers Georgia-Rae's advice and wills himself not to spit it all out. He feels his face going purple and the pot burning his throat but still he stubbornly holds it in. 'Okay, let it out now,' she says, and he blows a sloppy blob of smoke and saliva into her face. He hunches forward, choking and clutching his neck.

Georgia-Rae looks panic-stricken. She pats his back lamely. Luckily the coughing subsides and Kenny slowly begins to catch his breath.

'You okay?'

'Oh, sure,' he wheezes.

'Anyhow, at least I broke you in and spared you embarrassin' yourself in front of kids your own age. Imagine an episode like this – you keelin' over and hackin' up a lung in front of a gang of obnoxious teenagers. It woulda been the downfall of your social life, so you can thank me for sparin' you the humiliation.'

'Thanks.'

'You high?'

'Huh?'

'Are you high? Do you feel stoned? You know, *baked*?'

'No, I feel just the same, only a little nauseous.'

'I thought so. I didn't get high my first time either. It's normal. Don't be alarmed or nothin'. Anyhow I broke you in, so next time you'll be sure to get a buzz on.'

'A buzz on what?'

Georgia-Rae giggles. 'Oh, Kenny, you're so innocent.'

Kenny flushes with embarrassment. 'I'm only twelve,' he says.

'Hmm. You got a gal back home?'

'Not yet.'

'When I was twelve I had *two* boyfriends! Hell, I was shavin' my legs and pits by then.'

'Wow. None of the girls in my class shave.'

'I sprouted early, that's why. Got my period at eleven. But everyone grows at their own pace so don't you worry about bein' a little behind.'

'Do you have a boyfriend now?' he asks her, waving her smoke out of his face.

'I see someone casually. He works at the Piggly Wiggly in the fish department. I don't know if we have a future, mind you. It's hard to get turned on when your lover smells like shrimp.' She stamps out the roach and flicks it over the railing. 'To be perfectly honest,' she says, 'I'm still carryin' a torch for Pug.'

'Pug?'

'My ex.'

'Where's your torch?'

'It's a figger of speech, lamb. We was steady for three years, then one day out of the blue he told me we was finished. It was the fourth of July. He tole me he was movin' on. Dumped me right there under the spectacular fireworks display, just like that – Bang! No pun intended. I says, "Pug, who're you movin' on to?" And he says, "Maisy Pickens."'

Georgia-Rae sighs, the wound still raw in her heart. 'Course Maisy Pickens is a better catch. She has fake boobs! See Kenny, guys don't care about if boobs is fake or not, so long as they're huge and perky. You a boob man yourself?'

'Huh?'

'Never mind.'

Spin n' Win

GEORGIA-RAE SQUEALS as they fly past the Welcome to Mississippi! sign. 'Home sweet home!' she cries, pushing her head out the window to let her hair blow in the wind. 'Yazoo is less than 180 miles from here!'

'How many kilometres is that, Mom?'

'Times it by one point six.'

'Y'all have been swell,' Georgia-Rae says wistfully. 'I'm almost sad our journey together is come to an end. I never expected such hospitality from Northerners. No offence, but you Northern folk have a reputation for being, well, *cold*.'

'Two hundred and eighty-eight kilometres to Yazoo!' Kenny exclaims.

'Listen, I have a confession to make,' Georgia-Rae says. 'I ain't really from Yazoo City.'

'You're not?'

Georgia-Rae shakes her head. ''Fraid not. Actually, I'd appreciate it if y'all could just drop me off at the Hojo's in Batesville.'

'Batesville?'

'Yup. It's about twenty miles from here.'

'But why did you lie, Georgia-Rae?'

'Yazoo City seemed more glamorous; I wanted to be colourful.'

'You are colourful. You don't need to lie.'

'Oh yes, I did.'

'Why?'

'This is not as easy as I hoped it'd be.'

'What?'

Georgia-Rae sighs and gropes around in her knapsack. She pulls out a gun and points it into the front seat. 'I need all your money. Gosh, I'm sorry about this. Really, y'all are so special and trusting. Just pull off at exit 13. That'll take us right into Batesville. I'm meetin' Pug at the Hojo's on Swamp Street.'

Ara chuckles. 'Hardy har har, Georgia-Rae.'

'Joke's on you, Miss Ara. This gun is real, and it's loaded.' She waves it around to make her point.

Ara gasps. Kenny looks alarmed. 'But I thought you and Pug...'

'We're still business partners.'

'You lied!'

'This is the real world, honey. Surprise.'

'What about your father?' Kenny asks desperately. 'And Nam?'

Georgia-Rae shrugs. 'He dodged the draft. He's a cop in Alabama. Left my mom for a topless dancer with a clit pierce. Pardon my fran-say.'

'I wish you'd watch what you say in front of Kenny,' Ara scolds. 'He's only twelve, you know.'

'It's the truth. She *does* have a pierce down there – a gold hoop. Daddy told me. He was all braggin' about it, all proud an' shit. The thought of it gives me the heebies. Can you imagine pokin' a hole in there?'

'In where? In where?' Kenny wants to know.

'Curiosity killed the cat,' Ara snaps.

'Hey, turn here,' Georgia instructs. 'That's right. The Hojo's is just left off Highway Avenue.'

Ara eases the car into the parking lot outside the Hojo's. 'Like I said, Miss Ara, I need all your money. Just hand me that money belt you got around your waist. That's right. I'll take it all.'

'But it's all I've got,' Ara says quietly.

'Now that's a dilemma, ain't it? I'm sorry, but I don't got a choice.'

'I can't give you my money belt,' Ara says firmly.

'Please cooperate with me, Miss Ara. You're such a doll and I'm real stuck on little Kenny. Please don't make me kill y'all.'

'Give her the money belt, Mom!'

Ara reluctantly hands over the brown-and-beige pouch. She wouldn't do it if she was alone. She'd rather be shot than have to part with her stash. But for Kenny's sake she doesn't hesitate. Georgia-Rae snatches the pouch out of her hands. 'Thank you so much. You're a doll.' She unzips the pouch and pulls out a twenty-dollar bill. 'Here, honey,' she says, handing it to Ara. 'Gas money to see you right through till Louisiana.' She pronounces it *Leeziana*.

'Thank you.'

'Ah, what the hell!' Georgia-Rae tosses another ten into the front seat. 'Go buy yourself some coffee and tampons.'

She gets out of the car and starts walking towards the Hojo's. She stops after a few feet, turns back and waves sweetly. Her smile looks genuine. And then she's gone.

Ara and Kenny sit very still until they see a silver Camaro roar out of the parking lot and onto the highway. 'Did you catch the licence plate number?' Ara says.

Kenny shakes his head. 'There was an L . . .'

'Now what?' Ara says dismally.

'I guess we were just hit by friendly fire,' he comments.

'Beg pardon?'

'You said she was a soldier in your platoon, Mom.'

Arabella grimaces.

'I told you it was dumb,' he says proudly. 'I told you so.'

Ara had envisioned them singing merrily as they crossed the state line into Louisiana, but instead she is sad and disillusioned, almost ready to turn around and go crawling back to Roman. For Kenny it's not so much about losing the money. It's more about the way his faith in the fundamental goodness of humanity has been sabotaged. For Ara, whose faith in humanity was snuffed out long ago, it's the money.

They stop in Baton Rouge to put their last five dollars' worth of gas into the car. 'I'm going to call Dayna,' Ara tells Kenny at the Gas n' Munch. 'She doesn't even know we left Montréal.'

'She'll be glad. She always used to tell you to leave Dad.'

'She didn't like him much.'

Kenny follows her to the payphone next to the toilets. He folds his arms across his chest and leans against the side of the phone. Ara calls collect.

'Mom, where are you?' Dayna cries. 'Why are you calling collect?'

'I'll pay you back, don't worry. I left Roman and I'm on the road and we were robbed by a hitchhiker so I'm flat broke.'

'Whoa. Where are you?'

'Baton Rouge. We're going to stay with Grandma.'

'You left the Boob for good?'

'I think so. He gave me a day at a spa – Le Spa on Laurier – for my birthday. Only he got me the Bare Essentials Package instead of the Belle-of-the-Ball –'

'The who of the what?'

'Belle of the ball. So I came home early.' She lowers her voice then so Kenny can't hear. 'I caught him naked with Tanya. He was wearing a dog collar.'

'Ew. Gag.'

'It was traumatic.'

'I'm glad you left.'

'So am I. Everything was going swell on the road until I hit that skunk and then picked up the hitchhiker.'

'What would possess you, Mom? It's not the sixties any more.'

'She was alone and I wanted to help a sister.'

'And then she robbed you.'

'Kenny was so disappointed. He really liked her. I think he had a crush on her.'

'I did not!' Kenny whines, punching his mother's shoulder.

'Anyway,' Ara continues, 'she took my money belt and now we have nothing except the thirty bucks she gave me for gas which is all used up. Aside from that I have one American dollar in the glove compartment. Remember my lucky dollar? The one I found in the sand at Old Orchard beach?'

'Buy yourself a lottery ticket.'

'With my lucky dollar?'

'Sure. Go on and take a chance.'

'And if I lose?'

'You'll be no worse off and the dollar won't have been lucky after all.'

'You're right about that, I've got nothing to lose.'

'Guess who I saw on 46th and 8th yesterday?' Dayna chirps. 'Matthew Broderick! He still had his pancake on from the stage.'

'Wow.'

'And last week I saw Winona outside the Paramount Hotel.'

'Winona who?'

'Winona *who*? God, get a life, Mom.'

'But how are *you*, Dane?'

'Great. New York is crawling with stars.'

'Do you bring your mace wherever you go?'

'Most of the time.'

'Don't take chances, Dayna. Carry it on you at *all* times. You had the alarm system installed, didn't you?'

'Yeah.'

'Remember you can use your key to jab a mugger's eye out ...'

'I know.'

'And scream as loud as you can if –'

'I *know*, Mom.'

'I love you, Danish.'

Ara stares at the selection of lottery tickets on display in the Gas n' Munch. 'Which one of these costs a dollar?' she asks the clerk.

'They're all a dollar, ma'am.'

'Try this one, Mom.' Kenny points to a shiny green ticket with silver words like tin foil that say Scratch & Spin!

Ara shrugs, pays for the ticket and hands it to Kenny. 'You scratch,' she says.

Kenny hunches over the counter and scratches all six boxes with his thumb nail. His tongue pokes out of the left corner of his mouth like a minnow swimming out of a jar. When he's done he blows on the ticket to examine the results. 'Three wheels,' he says.

'Three wheels?'

'Yeah, we got three wheels.'

'What's a wheel?' Ara asks. 'What did we win?'

'Did y'all say ya got three wheels?' the clerk cuts in. Kenny nods. 'Congratulations!' the clerk exclaims.

'What did we win, for heaven's sake?' Ara's patience is stretched thin like pulled toffee. What's the big deal about winning a damn wheel? she wants to know.

'Y'all won a chance to appear on Spin n' Win!' the clerk explains.

'What's that?'

'Only the most popular game show in Southern Louisiana! It's on every weeknight at seven, channel four. WCAJ, Baton Rouge.

Y'all get a chance to spin the wheel on TV!'

'What about money? Can we win money?'

'That's the whole point, ma'am. Y'all can win up to five hundred thousand dollars, or a brand new set of appliances. You cain't lose, really. Y'all are guaranteed at least five grand.'

'Five grand!' Ara yelps.

'And we get to be on TV!' Kenny adds.

The clerk is laughing excitedly, as though the ticket is partly his. 'I'll be sure to tell everyone I know that that there winnin' ticket comes from Arty's Gas n' Munch,' he says. 'And that *I'm* the one who sold it to you! It'll really pump up business. Get it? *Pump* up business? It bein' a gas station an' all?'

Ara churns out an obliging laugh. 'Thank you,' she says. 'Thank you so much.'

'It wasn't nothin' at all, ma'am. Just a stroke of good luck on both our parts.'

Mama

THE FIRST THING ARA NOTICES when her mother opens the door is the way Melva Cusper Spurnicky's face has sunk inward like a failed soufflé. She's always been skinny but in her orange denim shorts and fringed halter top it looks as though she is being sucked in at the centre. Her flesh is flaccid in the thighs and underarms and she's underweight except for a pair of oddly firm breasts that look like the stiff peaks of beaten egg whites.

'Well, looky who's here!' Melva exclaims, her forced smile threatening to crack the thick layer of orange foundation on her face. She ushers them inside, asking them about the drive, the weather back home, Roman and Dayna, whether or not they want iced tea. The house smells of peach air freshener and cigarettes. Ara says, 'Iced tea would be fine,' and then, 'You're so thin, Mama.'

'Wish I could say the same of you.'

Ara forces a smile, resigning herself to the abuse.

They drop their suitcases at the foot of the staircase and follow Melva into the kitchen. 'Where's Nectar?' Ara asks, collapsing gratefully into a chair.

'In bed. He cain't get up any more.'

'You're getting a Southern accent,' Ara comments. 'Why can't he get out of bed?'

'He's sick. Got cancer in his throat. What did he expect? The man smoked three packs a day for sixty-seven years.'

'You hardly seem devastated.'

'Devastated? I've got a clock beside his bed counting down the minutes till he croaks. Stingy old miser. I've waited twenty years to spend his money.'

'Mama, don't talk that way in front of Kenny. Besides, you might be next. You've been smoking for as long as I can remember.'

'Never more than a pack a day and *always* Lites.'

Melva plunks two tall cups of iced tea down on the table. The cups are dark red plastic and look like stained glass – the kind they have at Pizza Hut. 'Here,' she says. 'I can add sugar if it's too bitter.'

Ara takes a sip and gags on the sweetness. 'How much sugar is in here?'

'A cup.'

'A cup? An entire cup?'

'I like it sweet.'

Ara pushes the iced tea away. 'Do you have water?' she asks.

'Course I have water. What kinda question is that?' She dumps Ara's iced tea back into the pitcher and fills the red cup with tap water. 'Did you leave Roman for good?' she asks.

'I think so.'

'The man's only human, Arabella. Maybe you're being too hard on him.'

'Please, Mama! He slept with my best friend.'

'He kept a roof over your head.'

'I want more out of life than a roof, Mama.'

'That there is your first mistake. High expectations can lead nowhere but down a path of disappointment.'

'We won the lotto,' Kenny announces. 'Spin n' Win.'

'You're gonna be on TV?' Melva bleats. 'Wowee! I can't believe it! You can win half a million buckeroos!'

'Dayna convinced me to buy the ticket with my lucky dollar. Neat, eh?'

'It's more than neat,' Melva says. 'It's fantastic.' She gulps iced tea straight from the pitcher, then adds, 'Y'all are welcome to stay here as long as you want. Think of my home as your very own for however long you like.'

Ara is no longer fooled by her mother's nice spells. She knows better now and thinks of Melva as a bitch in remission rather than a changed woman. With Melva, as with Roman, there is always an ulterior motive for kindness.

'I'd better go up and say hello to Nectar,' Ara says. 'Is he well enough for visitors?'

'Oh sure. He's probably crocheting.'

'Crocheting?'

'Yeah. He crochets women's sweaters. He's not bad either. They sell like hotcakes at the Clothes Horse on Vermilion. Be prepared, he has flatulence. Cain't barely control his bowels.'

Nectar Spurnicky, despite being almost eighty-five and bedridden with throat cancer, is surprisingly sprightly and energetic. He plants a fervent kiss on Ara's lips.

'You remember Kenny,' she says.

'Hey, kiddo! You sure have grown.'

'Hi, Grampa Nectar.'

Kenny hovers shyly in the background, faintly sick from the smell of stale farts. Ara immediately opens the window. 'Why doesn't Mama keep this window open?' she asks.

'I think she's trying to suffocate me.'

'What do you do to keep busy cooped up in here all day?' Ara asks, sitting down on the edge of his mattress. She notices that the mole on his chin is bigger than ever, at least double the size it once was. Funny the way old age makes all the wrong things shrink or grow.

He holds up a half-finished green cardigan, the rich colour of leaves in summer. 'I'm making a small fortune selling these,' he says proudly. 'It was your mother who got me hooked. Haha! That's my favourite joke. Hooked. Get it?'

'It really is nice,' Ara says, inspecting his work. 'Lovely.'

'They sell for $114.99 at the Clothes Horse, you know. Sally Thibodeaux just ordered another dozen. Not bad for an old fart like me, huh?'

Old fart is right, Ara thinks.

'But you can have this one for free,' Nectar says.

'Oh, Nectar, that's sweet.'

'It's the least I can do for my favourite stepdaughter. Especially seeing as how you're going through a rough time now.'

'I'll manage.'

'Of course you will. You deserve better.'

'Anyway, you're the one going through a rough time,' Ara says, gently patting his spotted hands. 'Mama told me about the cancer.'

'I'm eighty-four and a half. It's about time.'

'Don't say that.'

'Ahh. I'm sick of the scenery down here. It's time for a change.'

Once Ara and Kenny are done settling into the guest room, they head back downstairs to the kitchen for supper. They find Melva leaning over the sink, peering into a compact mirror and applying lipstick to her rapidly fading lips.

'Are you going out?' Ara says.

'I gotta go to work. You'll have to fend for yourself. I'm never here at supper so the fridge is pretty bare. I think there's leftover gumbo in there but it's at least three weeks old. Smell it first to be safe. You can order in fried chicken. There's a place on Jefferson that delivers.'

'What about Nectar?'

'What about him?'

'Don't you feed him?'

Melva shrugs. 'I bring him wings or po'boys after my shift.'

'He eats po'boys with throat cancer?'

'I purée them in the Cuisinart.'

'But your shift ends at two in the morning.'

'He's never very hungry.' Melva puckers her lips, inspecting the coat of lipstick she's just applied. Already it's bleeding into the lines around her mouth. She doesn't seem to mind. Maybe standards diminish with age also, Ara thinks, the way looks do.

'Have a good night,' Ara says.

'I doubt it,' Melva answers. 'Tips aren't what they used to be. My body's still in top shape but let's face it, I'm in my sixties. They just hired a new girl. Seventeen years old. A kid! How do you think she makes me look? There I am almost fifty years older than her and prancin' around with my titties bare neckid.' She slaps the compact shut and tosses it into a straw bag. 'But I still got it. People travel far and wide to get served by me. I'm something of a showpiece at work. My titties are as youthful and firm as they ever were, thanks to Dr Dubois.' She pulls up her halter top to display her breasts. The aureole is dark brown, the colour of raw liver, and although they are quite firm, there is something grotesque about them. Kenny winces and turns away.

'Mama, *please*,' Ara says. 'Not in front of Kenny.'

'What? He's never seen a pair of titties before? Heaven's sake, girl, I'm his grandmother!'

Ara sighs. 'I wish you'd quit that job and do something more respectable.'

'Respectable? When did you become such a snob?'

'I'm not a snob, Mama.'

'It wasn't easy for me, you know. After your father was blown up, all I had to support us with were *these*!' She points to her breasts in game-show-hostess fashion. 'And they did a fine job, I might add.'

'But you don't have to work any more. You haven't had to work since you married Nectar. Doesn't he take good care of you?'

'Oh sure, he takes care of me. But I hate having to beg for my spending money like a dog. Besides, if you want to know the truth I like the attention. I get more male attention at work in one night than I got in twenty years with that old thug upstairs.'

'But isn't it degrading?'

'Degrading? It's downright flattering, all those men commenting on my firm and youthful breasts. And furthermore,' Melva rages, 'you might end up doing the exact same thing in a matter of time. Now *you're* alone with a kid to support and you'll see how hard it is.'

'I've done it before.'

'Your first husband sent you a cheque every month, that's how you survived. Do you think Roman is gonna support you like that on his nurse's salary?'

'I don't want Roman's money,' Ara says. 'I'm going to find a job.'

'And don't forget the Spin n' Win,' Kenny reminds them. 'Maybe we'll win half a million dollars.'

'He's right,' Ara says defiantly. 'There's that.'

Melva sprays No Name hairspray into the air above her head, then dumps the can into her straw bag. 'You'll see, Arabella, what you won't do for a buck.' And then she stomps out of the kitchen, slamming the screen door behind her.

'Grandma sure is mean,' Kenny says matter-of-factly, when he's sure the old woman is out of hearing range.

'She certainly won't be baking us Toll House cookies any time soon.'

'You're not going to work in a topless bar, are you, Mom?'

'Only when pigs fly.'

Arabella takes the car to the supermarket on Johnston Street. She is always surprised at how flat and bland the city is. The most impressive thing about Lafayette is the size of its K-mart Superstore. It's only when she's travelled the few miles outside the city into the French towns like St. Martinville and Cecilia that she's ever felt like she was actually in Cajun country and not just any old American town. Ara can't wait to take Kenny on a swamp tour of one of the bayous. Maybe he'll get to see a live alligator. Last visit he was too young to appreciate the charm and character of Southern Louisiana. All he knows of the place is his grandmother's suburban house and the giant K-mart.

She buys a box of Uncle Ben's rice, a bag of onions, a stalk of celery and two pounds of fresh shrimp. She pays for it with the fifty-dollar bill Nectar gave her, so grateful was he to get a home-cooked meal at suppertime instead of puréed wings at two-thirty in the morning.

On one of her visits to Lafayette back in her college days, Ara took a course in Cajun cooking. It helped to pass the summer and she learned how to make a mean jambalaya. Now Kenny stands beside her and watches with great interest while she removes the shells from the shrimp. 'Why don't you ever cook like this at home?'

'I only get in the Cajun spirit when I'm down South.'

'Is it going to be very spicy? I'm sensitive to hot food.'

'I'll make it mild.'

'Nectar just told me all about the Acadians,' he informs her. 'They were deported from Nova Scotia in 1755 because they wouldn't pledge allegiance to the British crown.'

'That's exactly right, slugger. And they settled along the bayous.'

'How come Grandma moved here?'

'It was Nectar's idea. I think his sister came here to teach French in the early seventies.'

'Actually it was my cousin.'

Ara and Kenny spin around to find Nectar hobbling into the kitchen in his blue polyester pyjamas and bare feet. Ara is distracted by the wiry silver hairs that stick out on his toes in perfect coils. 'I thought I'd join you in here for supper,' he says, dropping with a thud into a nearby chair.

'Are you sure? We could all eat in your room.'

'My ass is numb from lying around in that bed all day. This'll do me good. It's been a long time since I've had a reason to come downstairs.'

Ara smiles at him sympathetically. She knows what living with Melva can do to a person.

'What happened was my cousin came here to teach French back when the government was trying to revitalize the language,' he explains, as a barely audible fart escapes into the air. Out of politeness, Kenny and Ara pretend nothing happened. Nectar continues. 'She came with a few other teachers from Québec and she fell in love with it. Never stopped talking about the Southern hospitality, the simplicity of life down here. So when I married Melva, I thought it was a perfect place for us to be.'

'Does Mama like living here?' Ara asks.

'If you want to know the truth,' Nectar confides, 'I don't think your mother would be happy anywhere.'

Just as Ara is scooping a second helping of jambalaya onto Nectar's plate, Melva bursts through the back door, throwing her straw bag onto the linoleum floor.

'What are you doing home so early?' Nectar says, looking up from his plate with disappointment.

'What the hell are you doing downstairs?' Melva snaps. 'You're bedridden.'

'I decided to get up. Don't worry, I'll live.'

'That's what worries me.'

'Mama, do you want some shrimp jambalaya?'

'I cain't think about eating right now. I was just fired.'

'Hallelujah,' Nectar mumbles.

'What happened?' Ara asks.

Melva pours herself a red Pizza Hut cup of vodka, which she keeps on the top shelf of the pantry, then lights a cigarette and joins them at the table. 'An hour into my shift,' she says breathlessly, 'the boss asks me to meet him in the storage room. I figure either he wants a blow job or I'm getting a raise. So he says, "Melva, you've been working here nearly twenty years," and I say, "that's right, Arty. Twenty years." So then he says, "All good things has to come to an end." Can you effin' believe it?' She takes a swig of vodka and follows it up with a hard drag off her cigarette. She blows the smoke onto Nectar's plate of jambalaya. 'So I say, "Arty, that's it? You're firing me just like that?" And do you know what he said? He said, "The customers are turned off by your shrivelled old body."' Melva buries her face in her hands and cries. 'My shrivelled old body! Can you believe it? Just when I was braggin' to you, Arabella, about what great shape I'm in. I don't think my body is shrivelled, do you?' She shoves the cigarette in her mouth so it dangles there between her lips, then hoists up her halter top for the second time that day. 'What do you think, honestly?'

'I think you shouldn't do that at the dinner table,' Ara says.

'Come on,' she shrieks, the cigarette bobbing up and down. 'Aren't my tits youthful?'

'They're fake,' Nectar says calmly. 'Anyhow, you're an old woman. What do you want, Bo Derek's body?'

'Shut up, you decrepit sack of bones. Ara, am I shrivelled?'

'No, Mama. Now pull your shirt down. Please.'

Melva sobs into her cup of vodka. '*All good things has to come to an end*,' she bawls. 'I never told you this, Arabella, but Arty has a sign outside the bar. Do you know what it says? It says, "Home of the Oldest Topless Waitress on the Bayou." Now that's something, huh?'

'You'll find another job,' Ara consoles her.

'But what about the prestige? I could have been in the Guinness book!'

'Yeah, right next to the oldest living whore,' Nectar mutters.

'Shut up, gut-rot.'

'Mama, Nectar will support you. Who needs a job at your age?'

'It's not the money,' she sniffs. 'It hasn't had anything to do with money for a long time.' She rubs the back of her hand under her nose. 'It was just good for my ego,' she sobs. 'A woman needs her self-esteem, and those men in the bar, that's what they gave me whenever they flirted with me or left a decent tip in my panties. And now it's all over. There's nothing left for a woman who's shrivelled.'

Le Ti-Cajun

FIRST ON ARA'S LIST of priorities is to enrol Kenny in school. She doesn't want him to miss more than one full week for fear it will damage the smooth and successful flow of his education. Luckily Kenny isn't fussy about what sort of school she chooses for him. He doesn't mind wearing a uniform or having just boys in his class or travelling an hour to get there on the school bus. He just wants to learn.

They plod down the deserted corridor of the Lafayette Middle School. In fifteen minutes, at 10:35 a.m., the bell will ring and two hundred restless students will burst through their classroom doors and spill onto the playground like water overflowing from a tub. Something about being inside an elementary school always gives Ara a jolt about her age. She imagines herself now, trying to squeeze her knees under one of the wooden desks and it makes her feel too big.

Walking by an open classroom where an elderly woman scribbles the multiplication table on the blackboard, Ara remembers how bleak and difficult her own school days were. She looks over at Kenny protectively and silently prays his life will run its course with fewer bumps and a lot more joy than hers did.

'I like these parquet floors,' Kenny comments. 'And there's a Dairy Queen next door. Did you notice?'

'You can get Blizzards at lunchtime.'

'Exactly what I was thinking.'

After a few faxes are sent from his old school in Montréal, Kenny is formally welcomed to grade six at the Lafayette Middle School. 'We're honoured to have you here,' the principal tells him. 'We're always glad to meet our Canadian cousins.'

Kenny smiles politely and is led away with a stoic expression on his face – a face too young for stoicism. Ara wonders if there is a twinge of sadness in his eyes or if maybe it's just nostalgia for his old life, which seems to be slipping farther and farther behind him. 'I'll pick you up at three-thirty,' she calls out.

And then he's gone, off to his brand new classroom. Ara sends another plea to God, this time requesting that Kenny not be scarred or damaged in any permanent way due to her sudden decision to uproot him. She sighs as she weaves her way through the parking lot, hoping that God can hear her, that she isn't impinging on His time.

She orders a plain vanilla cone at Dairy Queen and buys the newspaper from the gas station next door. She gets back into her car which is still parked in the school's lot and flips through to section C of her paper. The classifieds. She scans the page intently, only remembering to lick her ice cream cone whenever the ice cream starts to dribble down her knuckles. By the time the cone is finished her hands are sticky and black from the newsprint. She wipes them on a tissue from her purse and at the same time takes out a pen. She circles two job possibilities, folds the classified section in half and starts the car.

Le Ti-Cajun Gazette does not have a wide enough circulation to merit occupying one of the highrise buildings in downtown Lafayette. Instead the office is contained in a stout red brick house off Highway 10, right next to the KOA campground. The house shakes every time an eighteen-wheeler whizzes by. Ara knocks tentatively before noticing the handwritten sign Scotch-taped to the door. It says *Just come in*. She takes a deep breath, holds her chin up in the air and enters *Le Ti-Cajun Gazette* headquarters.

'Hello?' she calls. The walls of the front hallway are lined with the front pages of old issues of the paper, mounted and framed, with each date engraved on a small gold plaque at the bottom. As she moves down the hallway she can hear the faint sound of singing. The singing gets louder as she rounds a corner into the living-slash-newsroom. 'Hello? Is anyone here?'

'Delta Dawn, what's that flower you have on, could it be a faded rose from days gone by?'

Ara recognizes the song right away. It's an old song from the seventies – a song Ara hasn't heard since her college days. Her dorm-mates used to sit around cross-legged in the TV room,

LE TI-CAJUN

smoking pot and singing folk songs to Cindi Pritcher's twangy guitar playing. It was the sort of thing college girls did back then when
they couldn't get a date. Maybe they still do. Now Ara pokes her face
into the newsroom – which is just a living room with a lot of desks
and computers – and finds a motley group of what she supposes are
journalists sitting in a circle and clapping their hands to 'Delta
Dawn'. In the centre of the circle, sitting on a stool hunched over his
guitar, a white-haired man with a long braid leads the singalong. His
rendition of the song is off key and way too loud, but he has stage
presence. Ara leans against the wall with her arms folded across her
chest and waits.

The white-haired man, who is wearing a T-shirt that says Era-
cism, has the guitar pressed right up against his belly. Without paus-
ing to catch his breath between songs he performs a medley of John
Denver's classic 'Rocky Mountain High', the Eagles' 'Peaceful, Easy
Feeling' and Janis Joplin's 'Bobby McGee'. Succumbing to a loud
boom of applause, he graciously performs an encore before bowing
and returning his guitar to its case. His audience claps with great
enthusiasm. 'Back to work,' he says gently. 'We have deadlines,
gang.'

He spots Ara and comes over to her with his arm outstretched.
'Oliver LaChance,' he says. 'Editor-in-chief. How can I help you?'

'You're the editor?' Ara says, shaking his hand.

'I am. Believe it or not, music is just a hobby.'

'Really.'

'Do you like classic rock?' he asks her.

'I'm not really a music connoisseur.'

'*Everyone* loves classic rock. How about folk?'

'I'm of the opinion that folk songs are somewhat outdated,' Ara
admits.

Oliver shrugs. 'A lot of people are ambivalent about John
Denver. I find him therapeutic,' he says. 'Anyway the singalongs
really perk up the staff.'

'They seem to enjoy it.'

'What can I do for you?' Oliver LaChance wants to know.

Ara holds up section C of the newspaper. 'I saw your ad in the
classifieds,' she says. 'You're looking for a copy editor.'

« 65 »

'Are you a copy editor?'

'No, I have a bachelor of arts with a major in philosophy and I've been a housewife for about twenty years. I'm a very good mother but I suppose that's superfluous as far as journalism is concerned.'

'Do you speak French?'

'I'm perfectly bilingual. I just moved here from Québec so French is still very fresh in my memory. French grammar was always my forté in high school. I won the Maria Chapdelaine French Literature prize in eighth grade. Aside from that I'm a fair writer. I dabbled in poetry but never had the confidence to pursue it. Which is not to say I can't cut it. I'm sure I can. Plus I read the newspaper every morning. I'm up on current affairs.'

'We're not exactly the *New York Times*.'

'I'm not exactly Woodward or Bernstein.'

'The theme of my paper is French Louisiana. We report on everything relating to *les Acadiens*. We're trying to salvage the language. It's in dire straits, if you hadn't noticed.'

'A worthy cause indeed.'

'The pay is feeble,' Oliver says. 'We're really more of a family than a business.'

'I have no delusions of grandeur,' Ara confesses. 'I know my credentials don't merit much more than minimum wage. I care more about job satisfaction.'

Oliver LaChance smiles one of those enveloping smiles, the kind that sets your nerves at ease, lets you know you've got a new friend, someone you can trust. 'Welcome,' he says. '*Et bonne chance.*'

Ara offers to get started right away. Oliver, impressed by her enthusiasm, introduces her to Franny Bullock, the layout editor. Franny says, 'There's a basket of stories that need editing on your desk.'

'Which is my desk?'

'Your office is upstairs. Second floor, last door on the right. It's across from the bathroom but don't worry about the smell, we always spray air freshener. Field-O-Flowers.'

'I forgot to ask you,' Oliver says to Ara, 'do you know Mac?'

'Who?'

'Macintosh.'

'Who's he?'

'*He* is a computer. Are you familiar with it? Are you competent in Pagemaker 3.1? What about Word? Powerpoint?'

'Oh dear,' she stammers. 'Computers.'

'Computers,' he echoes.

'I've never used one before but that's no problem. If you could just show me how to turn it on I'll figure the rest out by myself. Is there a manual?'

Lucky for Ara she has a magnetic aura. Or at least large breasts. Ollie LaChance quickly develops a pubescent-style crush on her, which works to her advantage because he is more than willing to spend hours up in her office, hunched over her shoulder patiently teaching her Computer 101, and yes, sneaking the occasional peak into her generous cleavage. It's a sacrifice she is willing to make, despite that long-ago promise not to exploit her breasts for personal gain, which now seems outdated. The information Ollie passes on is very valuable. Within two weeks she is not only computer-literate but also dating him on the sly.

'How do you feel about taking your career in a new direction?' Ollie asks her over crawfish tortellini at the Bayou Bar and Grill.

'My career's only been going in *this* direction for two weeks. A change this early on seems hasty.'

'Hasty pasty. You've got talent, Arabella.'

'How do you know? All I do is correct grammar and spelling mistakes.'

'I need you to do a review of that new Indian restaurant on Pinhook Road.'

'I thought you only reported stories relating to French Louisiana.'

'I have a two-by-nine-inch gap on page four,' he says, flicking a piece of crawfish out of his beard.

'But I'm just a copy editor,' Ara reminds him.

'Well, now you're a copy editor *and* restaurant critic.' He affectionately pats her hand. She smiles at him politely but can't reciprocate the sentiment. Truth is she's not the least bit attracted to him. She has an aversion to ex-hippies – something about old men with long silver hair and braids. It gives her the willies. She prefers men who age gracefully and get their hair cut every month.

That first night when he invited her to see Tippy Thibodeaux at the Bayou Bar and Grill, she thought she might give Oliver a chance – he was so rosy and warm, why not? But by the second date she knew it was a no-go. He asked her how she felt about Kenny dropping acid as a way to 'expand his horizons' and 'diversify his perceptions'. She almost gagged on her catfish and decided there and then, as Tippy Thibodeaux sang his heart out on the stage, to avert a relationship at all costs. Only now she's worried about jeopardizing her job at the paper. She's not sure how long she can keep leading him on. She thinks maybe she should end it tonight, before the Bayou becomes 'their place'.

'I'll need the review by six tomorrow night,' Ollie says. 'Just do your best.'

'But I don't like Indian food,' Ara tells him. 'Isn't that an automatic bias?'

'Journalism is never objective. That's the first thing you learn.'

'It just doesn't seem fair to the restaurant's owners.'

'There's no such thing as fairness in journalism. That's the second thing you learn.'

'Journalism must be a lonely profession,' Ara comments, poking her tortellini with her fork.

'Lonely shmonely,' he says.

She never gets around to dumping him.

The Cajun Delhi, Lafayette's only authentic Indian restaurant, had two major strikes against it: one, the food smelled like cheap perfume, and two, the place was filthy. Her elbows kept sticking to the plastic table cloth and she had to return her fork because there was pilaf rice encrusted on the prongs. There was a wine stain on the beige carpet at her feet and an orange tabby that slept peacefully under the table beside her. There is something unsettling about animals in a restaurant, even an adorable cat she might otherwise have liked.

She is staring at the bright blue screen of her computer, aimlessly steering her mouse around on its pad. She is at an impasse with the review. On the one hand she doesn't want to encourage the members of her community, her *new* community, to dine in a restaurant with grease-spattered windows and sticky tables. She has an obligation to warn people.

On the flip side, the restaurant owners – a lovely family from Sri Lanka – were accommodating and polite, basically delightful and impossible to dislike. Ara does not want to be responsible for the bankruptcy of their business or the disintegration of their family dream. She is furious with Oliver for dumping this review on her shoulders.

She taps a few words on her keyboard. *Lovers of Indian food can finally rejoice over the opening of downtown Lafayette's first Indian restaurant...*

She stares at her lead, wonders if the word 'rejoice' is too dramatic for a restaurant review. A person might rejoice over peace in Bosnia or over the birth of a child, but over an Indian restaurant on Pinhook Road in Lafayette, Louisiana? She doubts it, but decides to leave it because of the time constraint. She'll correct it later, in the editing. Now she concentrates on the rest of the review.

The Cajun Delhi has a simple decor.
The Cajun Delhi is a modest little...
The Cajun Delhi is a little dingy but...
If you ignore the surroundings at the Cajun Delhi...
The owners of the Cajun Delhi are delightful...
Stay away from the curried beet soup...

She turns off her computer screen and marches downstairs. It's post-singalong and Oliver is just sliding his guitar back into its case while the staff disperses and heads back to their desks.

'Oliver?' she says. 'May I speak with you please?'

'You missed the singalong,' he comments.

'I've been mulling something over,' she says.

'What's wrong?'

'I know it seems forward of me and, believe me, I did everything in my power to avoid a confrontation, but I have to be honest with you. I'm no restaurant critic. I don't want to hurt anybody's feelings – especially not the Edrisinghes. They just moved here from Sri Lanka and I don't have the heart to tell the world that their curried chicken tastes like soap. So it's me or the restaurant review. You've got to choose.'

'It's a little early on in your career to be giving me ultimatums, don't you think?'

'I'm sure you're right, but unsolicited criticism just isn't in my nature. I'll have to quit if you make me do it.'

'What about us?' he asks her.

'Us?'

'Yeah. How will my decision affect *us*? As a couple I mean.'

'That's another thing, Oliver. We're not a couple. We never will be. I'm not ready for a new relationship and frankly I'm not at all attracted to you. But that shouldn't impair your professional judgement.'

'Gosh,' he says, taking a step back.

'I'm sorry,' Ara mutters. 'But I'd like you to make a decision about the review – about my job – without basing it on our failed romance. I'd like to stay on as copy editor and I do like the idea of trying my hand at reporting.'

'You're a tough lady, Arabella. A real heartbreaker too.'

It's a good thing Ollie LaChance is a fair man or else Ara might have found herself back in her car, scanning the latest section of the classifieds. Instead she returns to her post as copy editor with a clear unburdened soul. Franny Bullock gives the Cajun Delhi her second highest restaurant rating ever: four chili peppers. She loved it! The only restaurant ever to receive higher – the coveted *five* chili peppers – was Oliver's favourite restaurant, the Bayou Bar and Grill.

Gypsi

ARA DUSTS THE COFFEE TABLE around Melva's feet in an attempt to keep the living room as tidy as possible. Not an easy task with Melva sprawled on the couch, her feet stretched out onto the table, cigarette ashes falling around her like snow. She's been planted in front of the TV for the last three weeks, since the day she was fired from her job. TV seems to offer her some intangible solace. It's like that for some people – a reassuring friend who never asks what's wrong, just sits there and entertains tirelessly, hour after hour.

'Mama, you should find another job if you're so depressed,' Ara says.

'Yeah right,' Melva sniffs, changing the channel with her remote.

'It can't be doing you any good sitting around chain-smoking all day.'

'Mind your own beeswax.'

'It's not good for Kenny to see you like this.'

'He doesn't leave his room long enough to see me. What's he do in there anyway? He's such an odd little thing.'

'Kenny likes to read, that's all. He's just reading.'

Melva lights another Winston. 'It ain't normal. It's after school. Why ain't he watchin' afternoon cartoons? They got "Power Rangers" on channel 47.'

'He's mature for his age. Cartoons don't interest him.'

'He's odd.'

'He's a genius. You'll see, one day he's going to be a neurosurgeon or an engineer or something spectacular.'

Melva switches channels until she lands on 'The New Price Is Right'. 'This host is *much sexier* than Bob Barker,' she comments. 'Don't you think?'

'He's not my type. He's too sunny.'

'If blond hair, blue eyes and broad shoulders is too sunny, then I sure like 'em sunny,' she says, flicking her ashes onto the carpet.

'Hey, check the mail, will ya? I'm expecting my severance pay any day. Go on, it should just be arriving.'

Ara sweeps her dust-rag over the top of the TV. 'Anything else?' she says.

'Just the mail.'

Ara goes out to the mailbox in her bare feet, carrying the dust rag and wearing her pink terry-cloth robe, the one Roman gave her on their fourth wedding anniversary. She shoves her hand into the mailbox and pulls out a lone letter, addressed to her in Dayna's easily identifiable scribble. Ara rips open the envelope right there on the front lawn, looking like a fifties housewife with a letter from Publisher's Clearing House.

Dear Mom. Big News: I spotted Madonna running in Central Park last Saturday! She's got calf muscles to die for. I followed behind her entourage until I collapsed after the fourth mile. But I snapped a picture with my McDonald's camera which, fortunately, I carry on me at all times. What a coup for my portfolio! Now I can die happy and fulfilled.

I'm proud of you for walking out on the Boob. You deserve better. I hope Kenny adjusts okay. They say boys need their fathers but I think you're a good enough parent for two. Speaking of fathers, I spoke to mine last week. I called him collect but he refused the charges. I had to call him back and put it on my calling card. He says he doesn't mean to hurt me, but my very existence reminds him of how old he is and apparently he doesn't want to be reminded any more. He sounded depressed. Something about the university wanting to retire him. Poor Daddy.

Ara folds the letter up and stuffs it back into the torn envelope. The words 'poor Daddy' slice her heart in two. There is no love blinder and deafer than a child's love for her parent, Ara thinks sadly. She blots a tear in her eye with the dust rag and heads back toward the house.

At the door she notices a woman in a Harley Davidson T-shirt and black leather shorts striding towards her. 'Hello!' the woman calls, waving a bony white arm in the air. 'Hello, neighbour!'

Ara smiles cautiously.

'You're Melva's daughter,' the woman says, like maybe Ara doesn't know it yet.

'Yes, I am.'

'Just moved up here from Canada, I hear.'

'That's right.'

'Welcome to the neighbourhood,' the woman says, handing Ara a plate wrapped in aluminum foil. 'I'm not much of a welcome committee but I did bake you a poppy seed loaf.'

'Thanks. Are all Americans so hospitable?'

'I suspect it depends on what part of America you come from. Take New York, for instance. I doubt you'd be getting a poppy seed loaf if you'd just moved to the Bronx. New Yorkers just aren't that way. I know. I grew up there.'

'My daughter goes to college there,' Ara says. 'I worry about her terribly.'

'Does she have a can of mace?'

Ara nods solemnly.

'Then she might be okay. I'm Gypsi Libertella. Glad to meet you.'

'Arabella Slominski Boot.'

'Will you be staying with your mother long?'

'Maybe. I left home quite suddenly and I don't actually have a plan yet. My future is still up in the air.'

'Let's go inside so I can read your palm.'

'I beg your pardon?'

'I'm a palmist. I can predict your future.'

'I don't know –'

'Don't worry, I never tell the person if I see something awful. Supposing you're going to die next week, I'd keep it to myself. Unless it's something I can prevent, in which case I might face a brief ethical dilemma but I'd tell you anyway.'

'Wouldn't I notice it in your expression, if I was going to die? Wouldn't your eyes betray you if you tried to hide something like that?'

'Oh no. I'm an expert. Last year I had a customer who had six months to live – tops! – and there was nothing I could do about it. It was in his palms as plain as red ink, but of course he had no idea because most people don't know the first thing about their own palms. His life line just stopped dead in the middle of his hand. Anyhow, I told him he had a long, glorious and prosperous life ahead of him. I told him to enjoy every single day. Four months later he died of an aneurysm in his brain. Poof. Just like that. But maybe what I gave him was four last good months on earth instead of four more ordinary months of worrying. I gave him hope right up until he croaked.'

'It scares me,' Ara confides.

'Come on, Arabella. You need to know what direction your life is going in. It's imperative.'

Ara sighs and lets Gypsi Libertella lead her inside her mother's house. Melva is still pasted to the couch, thoroughly absorbed in 'Showcase Showdown'. 'Where's my cheque?' she asks absently.

'It didn't arrive yet,' Ara says. 'I'll be in the kitchen if you need me, Mama. Gypsi's going to read my palms.'

Melva rolls her eyes. 'You don't believe in that bull-poop, do you?'

'Not really,' Ara mutters. 'But if it'll help ...'

'It will help,' Gypsi promises. 'You'll see.'

They sit down opposite each other at the kitchen table. 'The atmosphere in here is a little antiseptic,' Gypsi says. 'Maybe we can light a candle.'

'Mama won't have any around. How about a flashlight?'

'That'll do.'

Ara gets up and rifles through the utility drawer, which has been steadily filling up over the last twenty years with every household piece of junk that can fit inside it: used Glad baggies intended for re-use, free samples of Sunlight dish soap, dead batteries, expired coupons, match packs, fridge magnets, loose change, five-year-old packs of gum, and a heavy box-shaped flashlight with a handle – the kind a miner would use to illuminate a coal mine. 'Here,' Ara says, handing Gypsi the flashlight. 'I don't know if it works.'

Gypsi flicks it on and is momentarily blinded. 'Batteries seem okay,' she says, blinking crazily as she props it upright on the table. 'Turn off the overhead light.'

In the stark white glow of the flashlight, Ara notices the word HOG tattooed on the inside of Gypsi's biceps. 'Why would you ever want the word "hog" tattooed on your arm?' she asks.

'Ever hear of Harley Davidsons? My old man is a biker.'

'Is that what he does for a living?'

'Heck no. He sells beaded car-seat covers for a living. But hogs are his passion.'

'I've always been afraid of motorcycles,' Ara says. 'They're so dangerous.'

'Sounds like you're afraid of life, Arabella. Now hand me your palms.'

Ara plunks her hands face up on the Formica tabletop. 'They might be sweaty,' she warns.

'I'm used to it. Now shush. Let's start with your life line.'

'Where did you learn to do this?'

'It's a gift, honey. You don't learn it.'

'How does my palm look?' Ara asks nervously. 'Am I going to die young?'

'You've got a good, strong life line. And it's long. Nothing to worry about in terms of dying young.'

'How do I know you're not just saying that?'

Gypsi shakes her head. 'Look here.' She traces Ara's life line right down to the wrist.

'That tickles,' Ara says.

'See how it wraps right around your wrist? Not even a crack in it. You might live to 110. Same thing with your fate line. It's a little faint near the wrist and right up into the middle of the palm which means you've had problems in the past, a lot of stress and worry. But the fate line is stronger near your fingers and that, my friend, means good fortune.' She pauses, and then: 'It's your head line that's a bit crooked.'

'What does that mean? Mental instability?'

'No, the head line predicts your career. It's full of cracks and tiny lines sprouting in all different directions. Like tributaries.'

'Am I a failure?'

'Course not. It means you'll be presented with different opportunities. You won't spend your whole life at the same job.'

'I just started one,' Ara says. 'I won't be switching careers again, will I?'

'I'm not exactly clear on that one.' Gypsi blushes. 'Palmists are only human.'

'What about love? Do you see a man called Roman Boot in any of those lines?'

Gypsi hunches forward, traces the heart line lightly with her fingertip. 'Two failed marriages,' she whispers.

'Wow, that's right.'

'Your mama told me,' she confesses. 'But neither of them was meant to be. I can see that by the two broken marriage lines right here.'

'I won't be going back to Roman, will I?'

'You're sure not supposed to, but that doesn't mean you won't.' Gypsi closes her eyes and rubs her thumbs into Ara's palms. Ara fidgets impatiently, shifts in her seat, looks over at the clock above the stove. 'Ara,' Gypsi says. 'There's only two marriage lines. You won't be a bride again.'

'That's probably for the best.'

'Wait –'

'What?'

'There's something …'

'Oh no.'

'A soulmate.'

'What?'

'You've got a soulmate.'

'Where?'

Gypsi's brows converge in concentration. 'How do I know?'

'Does he have a full head of hair?'

'Just be forewarned. He's out there somewhere.'

'You can tell that from the palm of my hand?'

'I can see the universe in here, honey.'

The Big Easy

OLIVER CALLS on a Thursday evening while Ara is working on the Jumble in the *Lafayette Chronicle-Herald*. It's a puzzle Ara has recently become addicted to, the object being to unscramble mixed-up words. The phone rings just as she is mulling over the word MOTRADO.

'Arabella, you're going to see Joe "Hooty" Birmingham,' Oliver announces.

'Joe Hooty who?'

'Joe "Hooty" Birmingham,' he says again. 'He's a sax player. He's playing Preservation Hall in the French Quarter all weekend and I want you to interview him.'

'In New Orleans?'

'Yup. Hooty's the only moderately famous musician we could get this year for our "Local Jazz Greats" feature. That and the fact he went to Lafayette High for a while.'

'Doesn't New Orleans have the highest number of murders per capita in America?'

'Don't tell me you've never been to the Big Easy,' Ollie groans. 'Heavens to Murgatroyd, Arabella, your mother lives in Lafayette!'

'I'm not one to seek out danger,' she tells him.

'Why don't you live a little? You know, *relax*.'

'But the crime rate is abominable there.'

'Have you ever tried a *beignet*?'

'A what?'

'It's a doughnut, Arabella, a fine French doughnut. Now I've booked you a room at the Maison Dupuis on Toulouse. You're right in the Quarter, a block away from Bourbon.'

'Oh dear.' Ara's adrenaline pumps through her veins. She's not sure if it's excitement or a panic attack.

'You can pick up his bio at the office,' Ollie says. 'I'll give you a map and directions.'

She decides to go as a fortieth birthday present to herself, a present that is long overdue. And this time she'll treat herself to more than the Bare Essentials. She'll knock herself out, really splurge. She doesn't need a husband to make her the Belle-of-the-Ball.

(Besides, now that Gypsi has predicted a long life for her, she doesn't have to worry about getting murdered in an alley behind Bourbon Street.)

Later that night she finds herself agonizing over the word MOTRADO. In the bathtub it finally comes to her. Doormat.

New Orleans is a deafening burst of laughter, an enclave of all that is wanton, corrupt, sensuous and tantalizing. It is the smooth wail of the sax, the fast tempo of zydeco in the sky. Toulouse, Bourbon, St Peter, Decatur, these are the performers' stages. In this town, the musicians own the streets and jazz oozes from the cracks in the sidewalks.

Ara jots it all down in her notebook, a souvenir for Kenny. She sips her café au lait outside on the terrace of the Café du Monde. Having succumbed to the temptation of three *beignets* she now wears a powdered sugar moustache. An old man with a black face crumpled like used tin foil plays the trumpet at her table. She taps her foot, smiling, and savours the taste of chicory coffee, the taste of freedom and renewal. Moments like these are scarce, she knows this. Maybe some people never have them, never feel the urge to smile for no reason. Ara knows that if she hadn't left Roman this moment would have evaded her.

Imagine. She might have lived her entire life without tasting a *beignet* in the French Quarter.

She finds a European chocolate on her pillow in the hotel. Her room smells of magnolia sachets. Real classy. Real France French. Ollie sure splurged, probably a last-ditch effort to woo her. Ara doesn't give a poop how much money he spent, she's just going to lap up every precious moment. New Orleans will do that; transform even the most conservative person into a primal, pleasure-seeking creature. Ara quickly falls under the spell.

She roams Bourbon Street before going to meet Hooty

Birmingham at Preservation Hall. She sips a lime daiquiri from a clear plastic cup, weaving in and out of the crowd. The smell of booze is on everyone's breath. Thanks to Eric, she has sensitive nostrils accustomed to detecting even the faintest trace of alcohol. Now it comes at her from all angles.

She drifts by a man with bleached white hair spiked straight up on his head. He twirls a sign in his hands – Live Orgy Inside! He holds the sign up to Ara, motions for her to enter his bar. She notices a photograph on the wall behind him – a knot of naked bodies on stage. She quickens her pace, looks away, but still wonders what a live orgy looks like.

There are bare breasts flashing from second-floor hotel balconies, transvestite strippers swinging their hips on street corners, tourists hunched over the curb puking. Ara thanks God she didn't bring Kenny along. She shudders at the thought of his innocence being stripped from him on Bourbon Street.

Just before the gay section of the street, Ara saunters past a voodoo shop. She slurps the last of her drink, tosses the cup into a trash can, and goes inside the store. The wooden floors squeak under her shoes. To her left there is a shrine to Marie La Violette. On the table where the shrine is laid there are dozens of candles burning in front of a creepy sepia photograph of an old woman. The table's surface is buried under a hill of coins – mostly pennies. A sign reads: Make your donation to Madame Marie and avoid a lifetime of bad luck.

Ara dumps sixty cents onto the table. She's had enough bad luck for one lifetime. If only she'd stumbled onto the shrine sooner.

'Believe in voodoo, ma'am?'

Ara spins around. A witchy-looking salesgirl is slumped against her cash register.

'I don't know much about it,' Ara admits. 'I'm from Canada. We don't practice much voodoo up there.'

'Anyone you'd like to off?'

'Off?'

'At least wound or maim. Revenge is very uplifting.'

Ara shrugs. 'Well, my husband's got something coming,' she says. 'So does my ex-husband, for that matter, and my former best friend. Also my mother's been getting on my nerves lately. If you want to know the truth there are *lots* of people who've crossed me recently.'

'You could use one of these.'

The salesgirl pushes her black hair away from her face and hands Ara a tiny stuffed doll no bigger than five inches tall. Its body and head are white and there's a tangle of black string (hair?) on its head. It has red painted lips in a crooked smile and two black marker slashes for eyes. There's a little red plastic pouch around its neck and four pins stuck in its belly. 'It's awful ugly,' Ara remarks.

'It's not meant to be cute. It's meant to be terrifying. See the red pouch,' the girl says. 'That's for the lock of hair.'

'Whose lock of hair?'

'Your victim. You've gotta have a lock of his hair or it won't work. Once you have the hair, you just poke the doll wherever you want to inflict pain. The deeper you poke, the more it hurts the person. Shove it right through the doll and bingo, he's dead.'

'Wow.'

'It's only ninety-nine cents.'

'I wouldn't mind giving Roman a nasty migraine,' Ara says. 'Or inflicting Eric with a backache he won't soon forget.'

'Go for it.'

Ara plunks ninety-nine cents onto the counter and grabs the doll. 'Thank you,' she says, tucking it into her purse and heading back out onto the throbbing pavement of Bourbon.

Preservation Hall is on St Peter. The air inside is dense and hot, opaque with smoke. They don't serve drinks or finger food, or anything, for that matter. It's just a stage and some chairs, packed to the ceiling with tourists as well as an unimaginable line-up outside. Ara squeezes into a space at the back of the room. She stands on tiptoe, trying to get a better look at Hooty Birmingham. She has a black-and-white photo of him from a couple of decades back – an unflattering publicity shot from 1975 – but he hardly looks like that now. For one thing he has short silver hair now instead of a big black afro, and the wrinkles on his face lend him an attractive maturity he didn't have in the picture. Besides, the seventies weren't kind to *anyone*. Ara leans back against the wall to focus (objectively) on the music. She isn't here to let loose and enjoy herself, she's here in the capacity of a journalist. Ollie says objectivity in journalism is an idealist myth, but Ara strives for it.

She thinks about taking notes for Kenny, maybe trying to describe the atmosphere or the music for him in her spiral notebook. But she decides not to. Jazz simply doesn't translate into words. On paper it loses its magic. Besides, despite her being a journalist she isn't a very good writer. Ollie says that doesn't matter. Most journalists can't write, he says.

Ara pulls a yellow cardboard disposable camera from her purse and snaps two pictures: one of the musicians on stage and one of the couple standing beside her. They smile and wave.

'Would you mind?' she says, handing them her camera.

They oblige and the woman takes Ara's picture and then they introduce themselves. They are Herb and Val Fitzhenry from Roanoke. 'I'm not a jazz fan myself,' says Val. 'I don't like music, period. But this place is supposed to be famous and my son said if I didn't come he'd never speak to me again.'

Herb says, 'I prefer show tunes.'

Ara drops her camera back into her purse and scans the room for a waiter or a bouncer – anyone who can direct her to the non-smoking section. 'This is unbearable,' she complains.

No one else seems to mind. The audience is in a jazz trance: eyes closed, heads bobbing, fingers snapping. On stage the music reaches a crescendo; people are standing up and whistling, others *whoop* their approval. Ara looks behind her and notices a crowd has gathered outside on the street to peer in through the open back door.

When the set is finished, Ara says goodbye to Herb and Val and makes her way to the stage. 'Mr Birmingham!' she bellows, her voice rising only slightly above the chaos. 'Mr Birmingham! I'm Arabella Slominksi Boot from *Le Ti-Cajun Gazette*.'

A slow look of recognition passes over Joe 'Hooty' Birmingham's glistening face. His eyes are like marinated olives, black and shiny. 'How you doin', *chère*,' he says. There is a French twang to his accent. 'I know of a quietuh spot.'

Ara follows him outside, back onto Bourbon and through the winding streets of the Quarter. He carries his sax case in his left hand. 'Nuthin' like playin' Preservation,' he says as they walk.

She jots that down on her pad: nothing like playing Preservation. She's not sure how it will play into her story but she'll figure out a way. You can never have too much information, especially quotes. Every good journalist knows that.

'How's right here?' he says as they come to a lone bench in the middle of Jackson Square.

'Oh, fine, I'm not fussy.' She sits down, crosses her legs and pulls out her camera. 'Smile,' she says.

He smiles.

'Now one with your sax.'

He lovingly opens the case and holds his sax up to his lips, pretending to play. Ara snaps the picture. 'Swell,' she says.

Hooty has broad shoulders, a sturdy physique and no sign of a protruding gut. He's not altogether unattractive, she determines.

'Let's start with the facts,' Ara says, businesslike. 'Your age?'

'Sixty-nine.'

'You're not!' she gasps.

'I do what I love, *chère*. It's the secret to preservin' my youthful good looks.'

'Goodness,' she says. 'You're like that Dick Clark fellow.'

'I do use an oil-based moisturizuh every night. But that's off the record.'

'Where were you born, Mr Hooty?'

'Just Hooty, please. There's no mistuh in front of it,' he says. 'I was born right here in the French Quartuh on the second-floor of a bordello.'

'A bordello?'

'Mothuh was a madam in Storyville, the old red light district. It closed down in '27 when they built the naval base across the watuh. I was just a baby.'

'Your mother was a prostitute?'

'A *madame*,' he discloses proudly.

'How dysfunctional.'

'I suppose by today's standards. But I grew up in a lovely three-story house on Bourbon.'

'A whorehouse?'

'When you put it that way ...'

'It just seems inappropriate for a growing boy.'

'But you're takin' it outta *my* context and puttin' it in yours. Oh sure, a split-level house in suburbia with an above-ground pool and a barbecue on the patio woulda been nice, but the white suburban folk weren't exactly welcomin' Negro prostitutes to the neighbourhoods. Anyhow, Ms Boot, I learned to play jazz in that bordello.'

'I didn't mean to imply –'

'Did you know, Ms Boot, that jazz was born in the bordellos of Storyville? In every parlour of those houses there was a band. Some of the musicians were self-taught, some of them had been schooled in Europe, but they all played togethuh, a mixture of different styles.'

'Jazz?'

'No,' he says, shaking his head. 'Blues. They played the blues downstairs while the women went about their business upstairs. Problem was, the blues weren't good for business. Too depressin'. The madams wanted somethin' lively and fast-paced, so they made the musicians play this upbeat skit-skat type stuff. *That*, Ms Boot, was jazz. Named after what went on upstairs, which was called *jas*.'

Hooty's voice is as smooth as his sax-playing. Ara lets the sound of his words swirl around her, lull her. She drifts into his stories, floats off with them, like being carried out by a gentle wave.

'Ms Boot?'

'Huh?'

'Aren't you gonna write any of this down?'

Ara glances at her notepad, which is blank except for the following: 'Nothing like playing Preservation' and '69 yrs!!'.

'Did your peculiar upbringing scar you in any way?' she asks, thinking of Kenny and wondering just how a boy turns out after he's had such an unconventional childhood.

'I don't recall mindin' much,' Hooty admits, scratching the tightly clipped silver curls on his head. 'All I knew was I had nine mamas.'

'Nine *hooker* mamas.'

'Do you know where the word hookuh comes from?'

'I'm sure *you* do.'

'In the old bordellos the experienced women worked on the

second floor. The younguh girls were on the main floor so to compete for business, the olduh women upstairs had to figure out a way to draw in the men. What they did was throw these fishin' lines out the window and reel in men's hats. That's why they was called hookuhs.'

'Nonsense!' Ara exclaims. 'You're toying with me.'

Hooty shrugs. 'History is whatevuh you wanna believe, *chère*.'

'When did you move to Lafayette?'

'Mothuh died from a rotting livuh. She drank too much. I went to live with an aunt at fourteen.' He leans his head back against the bench, looking up at the dark sky. 'I love this place. The Quartuh is rich with hidden possibility. Underneath all the noise and partyin' there's a layer of dange-uh. And then anuthuh layer of magic and mystery. There's so many layers you can feel them bubblin' under your feet.'

Ara shudders.

'Anythin' can happen here.'

'I bought a voodoo doll,' she tells him.

'Be careful,' he says. 'Some people don't know what to do with their powuh.'

'It's just a ninety-nine-cent doll.'

'Famous last words, suguh.'

She swats his shoulder as though to say, Yeah right! and then says, 'Do you think of New Orleans as your home?'

'Home? Now here's a cliché for your story, Ms Boot. Home is right here in this case.' He holds up his saxophone.

'But where do you *live*?'

'I tole you. I live in here.' He taps the case. 'But tonight I'm stayin' at the Decatur Rooming House, if that's what you're aftuh.'

'No split-level house in suburbia?' she says.

He tosses his head back and releases an explosive laugh. 'I'm too young to settle down,' he says. 'Where's your home, Ms Boot?'

'I'm still looking.'

'See, you're lookin' for somethin' that's actually right here.' He leans in to her so she can see the gel shimmering on his head and he touches her chest bone lightly. Then he squeezes her hand like they are old acquaintances.

Something about him makes her feel anxious and peaceful at the same time.

'Would you like a drink, Ms Boot?' Their outer thighs are touching lightly, just enough to send pinpricks travelling up and down her skin.

Melva once told her musicians were irresistible. She said they had a *je ne sais quoi*. For once her mother had spoken the truth.

'I suppose I'm a tad thirsty,' Ara says. 'We can continue the interview over a drink if it will help you loosen up.'

'Oh, I'm loose, Ms Boot. I'm loose.' He stands up and offers her his hand. 'Have you ever tried a Hurricane, *chère*?'

Voodoo Revenge

HOOTY AND ARA MAKE LOVE all night to the low hum of the heater and the faint shrieks from Bourbon Street. They make love in her queen-size bed with the smell of magnolia in the air.

Ara, who doesn't handle her liquor well, had two Hurricanes and invited Hooty back to her hotel. At the time a one-night stand seemed a perfectly logical development, sitting there in that bar in the Debauchery Capital of America. If you're not going to have your first one-night stand in New Orleans, where then?

Hooty makes love with his head, his heart and his soul – not just with his penis, like Roman did. He possesses the great gift of sensitivity, has more passion and sensuality in his fingertips than Roman had from his head right down to his webbed toes. Hooty's touches are electric and compelling. Her orgasm – the first since Eric – is like waking up from a long numbing coma.

'I bet you have a gal in every city,' she says with her head secured under his armpit.

'Oh sure, they call me "Don Hooty Juan".'

'I don't mind telling you that you were my first casual sex partner.'

He strokes her hair. 'That word, casual, it offends me. Makin' love is never casual, *chère*.'

'Now what?' she says hoarsely. 'Will we ever be together again?'

'Shhh. Why you gotta plan for the next moment already? We're not finished this one yet.'

'How do you do it?' she asks. 'Live in the moment like that?'

'I got the *joie de vivre*,' he says.

'I wish I had it.'

'You do. It's just buried under a lot of anxiety. People get brainwashed to believe they're not supposed to enjoy life.'

'But –'

'How can you be enjoyin' lyin' here with me now, if already you're thinkin' about sayin' goodbye latuh?'

'It's just putting a damper on things for me.'

'*You're* puttin' the dampuh, *chère*.'

'I like the way you call me that,' she says. 'It reminds me of Sonny and Cher. I always wanted to be her. She had a great voice and that really long straight black hair to her bum.'

Hooty laughs an even row of white piano-key teeth. Without saying another word he slides out of bed and creeps to the window; he opens it wide, then gently pulls his saxophone from its case and settles naked onto the ledge of the window. His black silhouette disappears in the dark, with only the golden sax reflecting the moon in its body. He plays for a long time in the window against the backdrop of a temporarily sleeping New Orleans. The music is haunted, lonely. Ara wants to take his picture then, preserve him as he is at that precise moment: naked with his saxophone, silhouetted against the city where he was born. But she leaves it. Some moments are better left alone, untampered.

She knows then that she has donated some vital part of herself to him. That night she dreams she is Cher, singing seductively on a piano while Sonny plays the sax.

Ara bangs on Gypsi's front door. 'Hey, where's the fire?' Gypsi pants. She is wiping her hands on her black leather chaps, leaving patches of flour like chalk on a blackboard. 'I'm baking pecan tarts. Come on in.'

Ara follows Gypsi into the kitchen. The counter is mostly buried under pie dough and pecans and the air smells like the bagel shop on St Viateur in Montréal. 'By the way, your poppy seed loaf was delicious,' Ara says. 'You bake often?'

'Every day except on Sundays.'

'I'm not much of a cook myself,' Ara admits. 'Although every now and then I get inspired.'

'It's my old man's birthday next week. I'm gonna bake him a hog cake! That'll be a challenge.'

Ara sits down at the table and draws a pensive breath.

'What's wrong, Arabella? Something on your mind?'

'Gypsi, you never said anything about finding him *this weekend*.'

'Who?'

'My soulmate.'

Gypsi pulls out a chair and sits down. 'Listen, hon, I never said I could provide an exact date. I'm a palmist, not a fortune teller.'

'Is there a difference?'

'Fortune tellers get more details. They also get more respect. Palmists aren't taken seriously in the business. But I wouldn't trust a fortune teller as far as I could throw one. But I did warn you your soulmate was out there.'

'I just wasn't prepared.'

'First of all, did you have a good time?'

'I had a marvellous time. *Marvellous.*'

'Well then,' Gypsi says, 'who needs preparation for falling in love?'

'He isn't what you'd expect.'

'What would I expect?'

Ara shrugs. 'He's older. Much older. And black.'

'I think he isn't what *you* expected,' Gypsi remarks.

'Maybe. He's a musician.'

'Oh boy.'

'What?'

'Trouble. Everyone knows musicians are trouble.'

'Not old jazz musicians.'

'You'll always come second in his life,' Gypsi warns. 'Music will always be his first love.'

'He was awfully fond of that sax.'

'Musicians are like bikers,' Gypsi laments. 'On a good day my old man'll show about as much interest in me as does his hog. But never more. There's always competition, hon.'

'And Hooty lives on the road.'

'*Hooty?*' Gypsi clucks her tongue. 'That's trouble.'

'He lives out of a sax case. Where do I fit in?'

Gypsi shakes her head. 'Damn musicians. You just can't tame them.'

'But there was this connection. I've never –'

'Don't waste your time.'

'It's too late. I've already fallen. I've never –'

'Stop it. How do you know he's the soulmate and not just some one-night stand?'

'Gypsi, a woman *knows*. In here.' She points to her chest.

'In your boobs?'

'My *heart*.'

Ara eats four pecan tarts and kills her appetite for supper. When Kenny complains about being hungry, she hands him three tarts wrapped in tin foil. 'This is what I'm having for supper?' he says. 'Three tarts?'

'Just this once,' Ara says absently, climbing the stairs to her bedroom.

'I'll have to brush my teeth twice before bed.'

'That's fine.'

'What vegetable will I have?'

'I think there's a carrot in the fridge.'

'Will you peel it for me?' he asks.

'Kenny, you're old enough to peel your own carrot.'

'What's wrong with you, Mom? You've been acting real strange since you got back from New Orleans.'

'Don't be silly. Now go peel that carrot and don't forget to wash it.'

When Kenny saunters off to the kitchen, Ara heads straight for her bed, closes her eyes and tries to conjure up Hooty's face. If she concentrates hard enough she can almost feel his skin, soft and worn like a faded leather jacket. And the way his black eyes twinkled like sequins the minute he put that sax between his lips ...

'Arabella? Hello? Earth to Arabella!'

Ara looks up into her mother's face. 'What is it, Mama?'

'Your boy is eating three pecan tarts for dinner. What's wrong with you?'

'I'm not in the mood to cook. It won't kill him.'

'Why are you so distracted? You've been locked in your bedroom for two days.'

'Why don't *you* cook him something if you're so concerned?'

'Ara, I don't like that tone. You know I ain't been myself since I got fired. I'm in a chronic depression. You and Kenny should be taking care of me, not the other way round.'

'Then go ask Kenny to cook *you* dinner.'

'So much for compassion,' Melva spits. 'You've just plain

abandoned this family.' And then she stomps out of Ara's bedroom, slamming the door behind her.

Ara closes her eyes again, calls up that fleeting image of Hooty as best she can. Now it's his smell that comes to her – bar smoke and Arrid Extra Dry. *I'll carry you in my case*, he told her in their last moments together, *right beside my sax*. Of course he wasn't speaking literally. What he meant was her spirit. He'd carry her spirit with him wherever he went. *What an honour*, she said. And then they kissed goodbye.

But they both agreed it wasn't a forever sort of goodbye. Maybe it was just his line.

Now Ara can't concentrate on anything for longer than two minutes. All she can think about is Hooty, Hooty, Hooty. 'Oh, Hooty,' she whispers, feeling like an achy teenager.

With sudden inspiration, she leaps out of bed and snatches her purse off the dresser. She finds the voodoo doll tucked into the side pocket and pulls it out, thinking that it took a man like Hooty to make her realize what a loser Roman is. Oh, she knew in her heart Roman was dull, insensitive and unfaithful, but she naturally assumed *all* men were such. Hooty proved her wrong. Hooty gave her hope for humankind in general, showed her there *are* gems in a great big pile of rubble. Her days of living in the rubble are *over*, and that was Hooty's greatest gift. That and the multiple orgasm.

In the adjoining bathroom she sits down on the toilet seat and rips a handful of hair from the brush she used to share with Roman. His hairs are easy to pick out; they're the silver ones with the white flakes attached.

Satisfied that she has enough for revenge to be effective, she shoves Roman's hairs into the pocket of the voodoo doll. 'God forgive me,' she mutters, and plunges four pins into the doll's head. 'That should give him one helluva migraine.'

Then she throws her head back and laughs.

Power

'I JUST WANT TO SAY that I'm proud of you, son. You've been very mature and supportive and if you'd like to visit your father at Thanksgiving, I'll gladly accompany you.'

Kenny shrugs. 'Do you think he'll want to see me?'

'I think so, slugger. You are his son, after all.'

They are sitting under the Evangeline Oak Tree along the Bayou Teche in St Martinville. Kenny has tired of searching for alligators and has joined his mother on the plaid blanket for vegetarian pâté with alfalfa sprout sandwiches and gumbo. 'Why is this tree called Evangeline?' Kenny asks, pointing to the gold plaque nailed to its trunk.

'It's named for the woman in Longfellow's epic poem.'

'Who's Longfellow?'

'He was a poet. He wrote about the legend of Emmeline Labiche.'

'Who was she?'

'She was a French girl from Nova Scotia, which, if you remember, was called Acadia back in 1755. Emmeline and her fiancé, Louis Arceneaux, were exiled with all the Acadians. But they were sent to Louisiana on separate ships.'

Kenny frowns.

'Louis arrived in Louisiana first and settled here in St Martinville, which wasn't called St Martinville back then but I don't remember what it was called. It took poor Emmeline three years to find him but eventually she made her way to this very spot.'

'Right here under the oak tree?'

'Yup. But it was too late. Louis had already married another woman.'

'Gosh, that's sad.'

'Emmeline died shortly after that of a broken heart.'

'How does a person die from a broken heart?' Kenny asks.

Ara shrugs. 'I'm not sure, slugger. I think the person must be so sad and so empty that it just stops beating.'

'Could it happen to anybody?'
'Not if the person is very strong.'

The phone is ringing as Kenny and Ara burst through the back door. Ara lunges for it, wheezing a breathless 'hello' into the receiver.

'Arabella?'

The voice is meek but recognizable. 'Tanya?'

'Am I bothering you?' Her voice is so small it almost disappears across the wire.

'I just got in,' Ara says coldly. 'What do you want?'

'I have some news.'

'Where are you?' Ara wants to know, imagining Tanya lying in her old peach chintz bed, wearing a black negligee and waving a whip in her pudgy hand.

'I'm in jail,' Tanya blurts.

'Jail?'

'I've been charged with attempted murder.'

'Murder?' The word hangs there ominously, heavy and dark. 'What happened?' Ara asks.

Tanya lets out a strangled wail, like a cat whose tail has been stepped on. 'I caught him in bed with one of the nurses he works with. A skinny middle-aged thing with pock-marks. Real low-class. You know the blue-eyeshadow-and-frosty-lipgloss kind?'

'So you tried to kill him?'

'I went crazy, Ara. I snapped. I grabbed his mini-golf trophy and smashed it on his head four times. He's in a coma.'

'Oh dear.'

'I feel terrible because of Kenny. I may have killed his father.'

'What are his chances?'

'The longer he stays in the coma, the worse they get.'

'Cripes.'

'Tell Kenny I'm sorry,' Tanya sobs. 'I'll probably spend the rest of my life in jail! It was a crime of passion. He provoked me!'

'Did you say you hit him on the head four times?'

'Yes, with his mini-golf trophy. You know the one he won in the Rotary Club tournament last summer?'

'Oh God,' Ara mutters.

'What is it?'

'I think *I* may have put Roman in a coma!' Ara slams the receiver into its cradle and bolts upstairs.

'What's wrong, Mom?' Kenny calls after her.

In her bedroom Ara digs through her underwear drawer until she finds the voodoo doll. Hoping she can reverse Roman's coma, she pulls the four pins out of the doll's head. 'I just meant to give him a migraine,' she mumbles to God. 'I honestly didn't mean to kill him.'

Kenny rushes into the room. 'What's going on, Mom?'

'Oh, Kenny, I have some terrible news.'

'Is it Dad? Is Dad the one Tanya tried to murder?'

Ara nods.

'Is he okay?' Kenny asks calmly. 'Is he gonna die?'

'I don't know, slugger. He's in a coma.'

'That's like sleeping but you don't wake up, right?'

'Sort of.'

Kenny brushes a tear from his left eye.

'We'll go visit him,' Ara offers. 'Whenever you like.'

'I'll need a note to miss school.'

'I'll book us a flight. I'm sure Nectar won't mind lending us some money.'

'How come you're holding a voodoo doll, Mom?'

Ara looks down at the doll. A chill ripples through her bones. 'It's just a souvenir from New Orleans.'

'It's creepy.'

'It is, isn't it?' She tosses it back in her underwear drawer.

Kenny spends the rest of the afternoon playing backgammon with Nectar, which seems to distract him from the bad news. Nectar has turned out to be a dear friend to Kenny and also something of an elderly father figure.

Ara encourages Kenny to have a good hard cry over Roman's misfortune; she tells him it's perfectly acceptable for a boy to cry when someone attempts to murder his father, that it's not wimpy or 'queer' in any way, but Kenny prefers to keep playing backgammon with Nectar. Ara worries about the way he keeps his pain locked up inside but she puts that thought on hold for the time being. More pressing is the voodoo doll in her underwear drawer and the possibility that *she* – not Tanya – is the real criminal who deserves to be locked up.

She dials Gypsi's number because although Gypsi is not traditionally educated, she has a lot of answers.

'Listen, I think you've hit the jackpot,' Gypsi says, biting into a chocolate cupcake topped with pink frosting. 'I mean, you have power now, Arabella. Major power. This doll is obviously authentic and it can do a lot of damage and it's in your possession. I just hope I don't get on your bad side.'

Ara licks the pink icing off her cupcake. 'I'm not sure I want that sort of power,' she says. 'I mean, if Roman doesn't pull through, that makes me a murderer.'

'You're wrong. This Tanya woman is the murderer. *She* did it.'

'But I made her do it.'

'Nonsense. You just poked some pins in a doll.'

'It's on my conscience.'

'Get over it. He had it coming and so did she. Now they're both paying.'

Ara sighs. 'It gives me the creeps.'

'Is there anyone else you hate?'

'Only my first husband. But I don't want to kill him. He's Dayna's father.'

'So wound him a little. You know, just use two of the pins instead of all four.'

Ara thinks about her last encounter with Eric at Le Spa. 'I don't know whether to help you or let you drown,' he'd snickered. The bastard. He'd even called her Babar. An elephant! And that smug, deprecating grin. And the way he hurts Dayna time and time again. Gosh, maybe this voodoo stuff is a blessing, like her own personal revenge kit. And who would believe it anyway? There's certainly no price to pay for the damage she causes, absolutely no one to answer to.

'But I don't have a lock of his hair,' Ara says. 'Darn.'

'Maybe your daughter can get some. Doesn't she visit him?'

'No, but I can. Kenny and I are going home to see Roman. No reason why I can't drop in and say hello to my first husband.'

'What are you going to do to him?' Gypsi asks excitedly. 'Jab him in the back? The knees?'

'Probably in the testicles. It just wouldn't be revenge otherwise.'

Gypsi and Ara clutch each other from laughing so hard.

Dear Mom, I got a first semester internship at Hot off the Press! *The editor was real impressed with my Madonna snapshot. He says I've got a bright future. My name may soon be in print.*

I hung out in front of Sardi's all afternoon yesterday but no one note-worthy emerged. Not a very fruitful week. My stake-out in front of NBC studios yielded nothing either, except a semi-obscure soap star.

I'm sorry about the Boob, for Kenny's sake. I don't want to sound cal-lous but being a vegetable hardly seems a regression from his former self. I say he's finally getting his just deserts. Send Grandma and Nectar my regards, and a kiss to Kenny.

Ara turns on the faucet and lets the hot water pour into her open palm. She dumps a third of a bottle of cheap passionfruit bubble bath into the tub and watches the suds fluff up until they are spilling over the rim. She pulls her grey sweatshirt over her head, slips out of her underwear and eases her body into the scalding water. Her shoulders slip under the surface of the bubbles. Her body feels like jelly, like you could spread her limbs over toast. It feels good. Life – despite the misfortune of her husband and ex-best friend, or perhaps because of it – has suddenly taken a turn for the better.

With her body immersed from the neck down in warm fruity bubbles, Hooty's spirit is close to her – the smell of his breath in the steam, his face there behind her closed eyes. On her best days, at her calmest moments, that's when he comes to her. When her heart is open she can fill up with him. He might have taken her with him in his sax case but she keeps him tucked safe in the strongest section of her soul.

'Mom?' Kenny's voice drifts in from the other side of the bath-room door.

'I'm in the bath.'

'Mom, I have to talk to you.'

'Kenny, I'm having a bath,' she says impatiently.

'Can I come in?'

'I'm not dressed, son.'

'Mom,' he says through the door. 'I think Grandma is poisoning Nectar.'

'Oh, shoot,' she mutters.

'I saw her pour Liquid Plumm'r in his eggshake.'

Ara sits up and pulls out the stopper to empty the tub. She reaches for a towel, watching the bubbles swirl down the drain. Hooty goes with them.

She finds Melva in the kitchen heating up a can of chunky soup and smoking a cigarette. 'Mama?' Ara says meekly.

Melva turns around, the cigarette dangling from her tangerine-coloured lips. 'Want some soup?' she asks.

Ara shakes her head.

'How about a Louisiana Lullaby?'

'What's that?'

'One and a half ounces of Jamaican rum, two teaspoons of Dubonnet and a splash of Grand Marnier.' She smiles crookedly. 'I'm gonna study bartending. Melva Cusper isn't finished with a career yet.'

'Mama, Kenny saw you pour Drano –'

'Liquid Plumm'r,' he corrects.

'He saw you pour Liquid Plumm'r into Nectar's milkshake.'

'He's fibbin'.'

'I saw you,' Kenny argues. 'I told Nectar too, so don't expect him to die.'

'You told him?' Melva snaps. 'I only put a teensy bit, to clean out his system. He's all clogged up inside. He's rotting and stinking up my whole house. It was just to clean him out a bit, I swear.'

'Mama, you can't feed him cleansing agents. It could kill him.'

'Really?' Melva gasps. 'Oh, horror! I didn't know.'

'Kenny, go upstairs and crochet with Nectar,' Ara says.

He frowns and skulks out of the kitchen. When she can hear him going up the stairs she turns back to her mother. 'Mama, you're not trying to kill him, are you?'

Melva drags her pot of soup off the stove. 'Arabella, he's as close to dead as any living human being can be. What's a little Liquid

Plumm'r gonna do? I call it Youth in Asia.'

'Mama!'

'Ara, you don't know what that cheap old miser has done to me all these years. Bossing me around, using his money to get blow jobs. He thinks his money gives him power over me. Well, he's just a withered sack of bones now and I'm the one with the upper hand.'

'Mama, you married him for his money so don't go blaming him for using it against you. It's your own fault.'

'Figures you'd side with him. He has the power over you too, can't you see? Without him you and Kenny would be starving.'

'He has no power over me,' Ara says. 'He's just generous, Mama. That's all.'

'That's always been your problem,' Melva hisses. 'An inability to recognize the people who manipulate you.'

'People don't manipulate me,' Ara protests limply.

'Ha. You're like a violin and everybody has played you. Including half-dead Nectar!'

'That's cruel.'

'Look at the fine mess you're in! Your life is in shambles because you always fail to see the way people use you. You hand over the power too easy.'

Ara shakes her head but can't find her voice to speak. She imagines her body as a violin with her head sitting stupidly on the violin's neck and she knows there is truth in what her mother is saying, and she also knows her mother is playing her right now.

Home

THE HOSPITAL WALLS are painted light blue, the colour of Crest toothpaste. It's a colour Ara has always found abrasive and it does little to improve the general atmosphere of the Queen Elizabeth Hospital.

Kenny trails along behind, nibbling the Planter's peanuts he got on the airplane. The flight attendant took a liking to him and gave him two extra bags as he deboarded. 'Hurry up,' Ara says.

He quickens his pace and catches up to his mother. They pause outside room 214 and collect themselves, neither of them sure what to expect. It's their first live coma.

Ara gently pushes open the door and pokes her head in to assess the situation before exposing Kenny to it. The room is dark with heavy turquoise curtains drawn to keep out even the narrowest sliver of light. Roman lies very still on his bed, his breathing even but unusually loud. His head is shaved bald and three-quarters of it is swathed in bandages. He looks asleep.

Kenny tiptoes into the room and stands for a long time beside his father without saying a word.

'You can tell him hello,' Ara says softly. 'They say people in comas can still hear.'

Kenny looks thoughtful. 'Hi, Dad,' he says. Then he shrugs helplessly and looks up at Ara. 'I don't know what else to say. We didn't talk much.'

'Just hold his hand, champ. He'll know you're here.'

Kenny picks up his father's limp hand and stands there with it awkwardly. 'I'm hungry,' he says quietly. 'Maybe we can come back after supper with Dayna.'

Ara pats his head lovingly. His hair is dirty from the plane ride but still soft. 'How about Chinese?' she says.

Dayna's train comes in at 8:05 that night. She strides through the station with a duffel bag flung over either shoulder, her blond hair bouncing like a seventies *Breck* girl. Ara always forgets how beautiful she is. 'How did I ever create her?' Ara wonders aloud. 'So confident and gorgeous. Where does it come from?'

Kenny shrugs. 'I don't think she's gorgeous.'

'You're her brother.'

Ara waves her arm at Dayna, who quickens her pace when she spots them. 'Danish,' Ara cries. 'You tinted your hair. It's adorable.'

'Highlighted. It gets so dark in the winter.'

'You always look gorgeous.'

'I wanted a golden hue. Like Jennifer Aniston. You know, from "Friends". It's very Manhattan.'

'Friends?'

'It's *the* show. What do you think about Melanie and Antonio?' Dayna asks, as the three of them walk arm in arm out to the car.

'Who's he? Antonio who?'

'Banderas, Mom. Haven't you heard?'

'What?'

'It's like you live in a cave or something. Melanie Griffith and Antonio Banderas! For God's sake, it's *the* hot fling.'

'I thought she was married to the "Miami Vice" guy?' Ara says ignorantly.

Dayna rolls her eyes. 'Yeah, and pastels are still in,' she says flippantly. 'Hel*looo*!'

They drive straight to the hospital with Dayna chatting energetically about Sarah Jessica Parker, Melanie Griffith and Pamela Anderson. 'I think it's dangerous,' she says. 'Silicone implants could very well be a modern plague of sorts for the Hollywood bimbo.'

'I'm glad you're here,' Ara tells Dayna. 'It was nice of you to come.'

Regardless of any animosity between them, Dayna knows it was her duty to pay Roman a visit out of loyalty to her little brother. Ara is grateful for her daughter's scruples.

'He looks so pitiful,' Dayna remarks.

'Shh. He can hear you,' Kenny whispers.

'Do you think he'll ever come out of this?'

'They say Tanya whacked him real hard. Hard enough to do permanent damage. She's a very strong woman.'

'She did this with a mini-golf trophy?'

'It was very pointy. The police have it now.'

'Can I be alone with him for a few minutes?' Kenny asks. Ara is startled. 'Just a few minutes,' he assures her.

'Of course, sweet-pea. We'll wait outside.'

Ara and Dayna leave the boy alone with Roman.

'Why do you think he wants to be alone with him?' Dayna asks, buying herself a cup of black coffee from the vending machine.

'Since when do you drink coffee?'

'All students do. Anyway, Roman never gave a hoot about Kenny. Why does Kenny care so much about bonding all of a sudden?'

'Roman's probably a better father when he's in a coma.'

'Good fathers are hard to come by,' Dayna says, then blows on her steaming coffee.

Ara reaches for her daughter's hand. 'I'm sorry,' she says. 'I failed both of you when it came to choosing your fathers.'

'Why is it so hard for Daddy to love me?'

'He's selfish.'

'Aren't we all?'

'You cramp his style,' Ara says. 'You know he likes to pretend he's thirty.'

'But he's in his seventies!'

'I understand how you feel,' Ara says. 'I was abandoned by my father too.'

'Mom, your father was blown up in a pizza joint. He couldn't exactly help it.'

'But it amounted to the same thing. He wasn't there.'

'But my father *chooses* not to be here.'

'Eric loves you in his own way,' Ara promises. 'Just like Roman – despite being comatose – loves Kenny.'

Dayna is unconvinced. 'Like many showbiz progeny,' she says, 'I have a deadbeat dad who prefers the company of women his daughter's age to the company of his own daughter.'

Ara squeezes Dayna's hand urgently. 'He won't get away with treating you this way,' she promises. 'I won't let him get away with this.'

Ara pounds on the door, furious. Egged on by her conversation with Dayna, by the sadness in Dayna's heart and the burden of rejection she has to bear every day, Ara dropped the kids off at the house and sped away on her mission of revenge.

'Who is it?' Eric calls from inside. 'Aurora?'

'It's me!' Ara shrieks.

Eric pulls open the door, frowning. 'You,' he croaks. 'Why are you still tormenting me?'

Ara's breath catches in her throat, feels like an ice cube that slid down by mistake. 'My God,' she gasps. 'You look so old.'

Eric snorts and lets her inside. He is stooped and withered, deflated like a flat tire. The golden Maurice Poupée hair piece, which somehow managed to slice a good ten years off his age, is gone now. Exposed is his red freckled scalp marred by age spots and decorated with only a few lone strands of white hair. His shoulders slump forward as though he is bending down to pick something up off the floor. His skin has a grey pallor and the defeated sunken quality of someone who is ill. He has aged decades since their last reunion.

'To what do I owe this visit?' he says, dropping heavily into a white rattan chair.

'Where's Aurora?'

'Aurora's gone. She left me.'

Ara sits down on the navy corduroy sofa. 'Better replace her quick,' she says. 'I hear Anna Nicole Smith is available.'

'Touché,' he mutters.

'I'm sure you can find yourself another student. You're not fussy as long as she was born after Watergate.'

'I don't have any more students.'

'Why not?'

'I was retired. Forced out. They're ridding the faculty of old geezers and I was the first to go.'

'Sorry.'

'Oh, sure. I can see the sympathy seeping from your pores.'

'Why did Aurora leave?'

'Look at me, Arabella. I'm old. She was young. It was inevitable. My bones crack, I'm impotent, I smell like mothballs, I fall asleep in mid-conversation and I need a walker. Would *you* want me?'

'You're impotent?' Ara squeals, delighted. 'There *is* a God.'

'I figured you'd gloat.'

'I have a right.'

'It's undignified.'

Ara chuckles. 'Speaking of dignified, where's your Maurice Poupée toupée?'

'What's the point?' he sighs. 'I'm already on the downward spiral to death.'

'Your optimism is refreshing.'

'Old age is not a time for optimism,' he mutters. 'I'm at the end, Arabella. I can smell it, the rotting odour of a corpse. *My* corpse! I'll be lucky to squeeze in another few years. Why bother with toupées?'

'A woman your age might find you attractive.'

'I'm not after a seventy-year-old woman. I never wanted a life partner to grow old with,' he says. 'I never wanted a granny for a wife.'

'And now you have no one.'

'I wouldn't live my life differently if I had it to do over.' He blows his nose into the handkerchief he keeps in the pocket of his velour robe.

'Did she leave you a note?'

'Who?'

'Aurora.'

'Oh, no, she told me to my face,' he says wearily. 'I believe her exact words were, "I find you repugnant".'

Ara giggles.

'Besides, she's found a younger man.'

'How young?' Ara asks, relishing each delicious detail.

'Sixty. She has a penchant for that age. Something about men being in a sexual renaissance at sixty.'

'Hm. We get menopause and men get a renaissance.'

'*My* renaissance has certainly run its course,' he laments. 'How's Dayna? I suspect that's why you're here.'

'She's in town. I think she'd like to see you.'

'I can't see her. I look awful.'

'She's your daughter, Eric. She won't care how you look.'

'I'd rather her remember me the way I used to be, when I could straighten my spine and work for a living.'

'She just wants to see you.'

'I'm too embarrassed, Ara. I'm sickly and grotesque. Who would want me as a father?'

'Dayna does.'

Eric shakes his head. His eyes are watery, bleak. 'Next time,' he says. 'When I'm not so depressed.'

'She's here *now*,' Ara says, standing up and straightening out her denim skirt. 'And you're not going to get any younger.'

'Yes, well ...'

'She's all you have to show for your seventy-two years on earth.'

'Don't remind me.'

'You're a pathetic man.'

'Tell me something I don't know.'

'I don't mean physically pathetic,' Ara fires.

'Neither do I.'

'Dayna deserves better.'

'As did you.'

'Humility doesn't become you,' Ara says. 'And neither does that velour robe. You look like Vincent Price.' With those parting words she leaves him slumped in his rattan chair, alone, consumed with self-pity and looking a thousand years old.

But first she excuses herself and goes to the bathroom. She finds his brush on the sink – the same one he had when they were married, with the fake wood handle and hard black bristles. There is one lone strand of silver hair wrapped around a bristle which she takes and wraps in toilet paper. She stands in the bathroom for a long time, looking down at the brush and contemplating whether she still feels a need for revenge. Along with his sex organ, Eric has also lost his arrogance. Any further acts of vengeance now seem superfluous.

Superfluous, yet *so* sweet.

Deadbeats

ARA STROKES KENNY'S HAIR and hums a lullaby, the way she used to when he was a baby. He is curled on his side, facing her with his eyes wide open. His old room is exactly as it was when they left, with pictures from *National Geographic* Scotch-taped to the walls and jars of dead insects lined up on the shelves. He's hardly looked at them since he's been back. It's as though he's a guest, staying in a stranger's bedroom, and he dare not touch that boy's belongings. That or they hold absolutely no interest for him.

'It's perfectly acceptable if you want to cry,' she says lightly.

Kenny blinks, dry-eyed. 'I don't want to,' he says evenly.

'Why not?'

'Dad wouldn't like it. He thought crying was for sissies. Remember?'

'This is different. I don't think he'd mind this time.'

'Crying is queer.'

'Is that why you're being so resilient?' Ara asks him.

'Maybe I'm just not sad,' he says, and she isn't able to read past his flat voice or his expressionless stare. She isn't able to read him any more and she's scared. She feels helpless, like she's only got a thin grasp on him and he's falling. She feels something like panic deep in her belly.

'Good night,' he says, and rolls over onto his other side. His back is like a new enemy.

In her own bedroom, the peach chintz bedroom of her past, Ara inspects everything with a fine-tooth comb for traces of Tanya or kinky sex or both. The bed is made, although not the way Ara used to make it. Instead the bedspread is pulled *over* the pillows. Ara used to show her pillows, which were always covered in crisp ruffled shams. There is no sign of these shams now. Maybe Tanya didn't like them. She is not a frilly-ruffly person. Ara wonders vaguely if Tanya washed the sheets and made the bed after attacking Roman with the mini-golf trophy. How else can one explain the conspicuous lack of blood and disarray?

Ara sits on the edge of the bed and replays in her mind the way she found them: Roman in that dog collar and Tanya curled up in his arms, naked and obese; then Tanya asking ever so sweetly if Ara had had a facial. Ara is suddenly determined to find the dog collar. She springs off the bed and starts ransacking the place, opening drawers, looking under the bed, sifting through the closet. Where is it? She dashes into the bathroom and searches the medicine cabinet. No sign of it. It seems that Tanya anticipated Ara's every move and rid the place of all incriminating evidence, all signs of their sleazy sexual encounters.

In a last effort to find the dog collar, Ara goes to the linen closet just outside the bedroom. The first thing she notices is that her best cotton percale sheet set with the embroidered edging is missing. She wonders if Tanya stole it, or worse, threw it out because of blood-stains. Then she feels something peculiar wrapped in an odd pillow case. She sticks her hand inside and pulls out a plastic eye mask, the Lone-Ranger kind the kids used to wear at Halloween. At the back of the closet she finds a black plastic brassiere, size 40 DD, and a ping-pong racket. And then she finds the dog collar carefully concealed in the folds of a fitted sheet, along with a leash and a plastic bone.

She packs all these things into the pillow case, not yet sure what to do with the bundle but positive it will come in handy at a later date.

She finds Dayna sprawled on the floor of the den watching 'Entertainment Tonight'. 'Hi,' Ara says, sitting down cross-legged on the floor.

'Hi, Mom. Did you know Rosie O'Donnell adopted a baby?'

Ara has no idea who Rosie O'Donnell is and doesn't much care. She nods politely.

'It's a good idea for an in-depth feature,' Dayna says. 'Famous actress-slash-comedienne adopts a baby. Did her fame facilitate the procedure? It's a hot new trend among Hollywood's elite, you know. Adoption is a viable alternative to getting fat for nine months and having to put your career on hold. It's food for thought, isn't it?'

'Why are you so obsessed with these people's lives? It's not reality, Dane.'

'Who says? Famous people are human beings as much as you or I.'

'Barely.'

'They're just more recognizable.'

'Their lives are fantasies and yet you care more about them than you do about your real friends.'

'Who's "real" anyway?'

'The people who go to college with you, for starters. Where are they? Don't you like any of them? Aren't there nice girls in your dorm?'

'They bore me. I haven't got time for that sort of buffoonery.'

'You'd rather devote your life to icons and illusions?'

'Icons and illusions. What a great title for a feature!'

'You're missing my point. I'm worried about you. You inhabit a world of make-believe.'

'I'm just devoted to my career,' Dayna says. 'I'm not some weirdo, Mom.'

Ara leans over and touches Dayna's cheek. 'I worry that I've been a bad mother and that's why you don't form relationships with real people.'

'I'm just quirky,' Dayna explains. 'Like Johnny Depp.'

'What will you do about your father while you're here?'

'Daddy's a lot like Hugh Hefner. You know, the aging Lothario in a velour robe. He'd sell his soul to put the skids on getting old.'

'You've been to see him.'

'I went this afternoon. He wasn't exactly thrilled to see me. I think he was expecting Horrora.'

'She left him.'

'I gathered. He looks awful, like an old man, despite all his efforts to the contrary.' Dayna turns off the TV with the remote control. 'Do you think he really loved Aurora?'

'No. It was her youth. That's what it's always about for him.'

'He gave me a text book,' Dayna says. '*Hero of Warsaw: The Life of Jozef Pilsudski*.'

'His favourite.'

'There's an inscription to me. It's quite touching.' She pulls the book out of her knapsack, which is lying on the floor beside her, and hands it to Ara.

It says: *Dear daughter, We all need heroes. I haven't been much of one to you but in my own peculiar way, I love you. Eric Slominski (your father).*

'Dear daughter?' Ara says, closing the book and passing it back to Dayna. 'What is this, the eighteenth century?'

'He tried.'

Ara snorts contemptuously.

'I feel sorry for him, Mom, and I love him.'

'You do?'

Dayna nods, turning the TV back on. 'He's human,' she says. 'We all are.'

Ara touches her daughter's cheek. She thinks it is truly amazing the way you can learn from your own offspring, from the very children you raised and taught yourself.

She goes upstairs and locks herself in the bathroom. She retrieves the piece of toilet paper that contains Eric's single strand of hair and drops the hair into the sink. She runs the cold water and watches it slide down the drain.

The next morning with both her children in tow, she marches down the hospital corridor to Roman's room carrying her pillow case filled with sex toys. 'Wait here,' she tells them and goes inside. Roman is exactly as she left him the day before, very still and blank like a corpse except for sporadic breaths that taper off into nothingness. 'I know you can hear me,' she says, dumping the pillow case on his belly. 'I brought some things that might jog your memory.'

One by one she pulls out her toys: the plastic bra, the ping-pong paddle, the Lone-Ranger mask, the dog bone, the leash. Finally she pulls out the dog collar and waves it in the air above his face. 'Remember this, Marmaduke?'

There is no response, not even the flicker of an eyelid.

'Arf, arf,' she taunts.

Nothing.

'Well, *I* remember and that's why you're here. It's not even about what you did to me,' she explains, as though he can hear her. 'It's what you did to Kenny – indirectly with your infidelity, and directly by being such a lousy father. Before this happened Kenny did everything he could to rebel against you. But now he's different. Suddenly he cares what you think of him. He wants to be a son you'd be proud of,' she says, picking up the dog collar and dangling it under his nose. 'Now that's something to strive for, isn't it?'

She drops the dog collar on his chest and walks out of the room.

Death & Rebirth

SINCE ROMAN'S ACCIDENT Ara dreams of death almost every night – her own death, Roman's death, even Eric's death. The dreams are vivid, real. Usually she wakes up with wet patches on the armpits of her nightgown. Sometimes she cries, 'Mama,' other times she says nothing. She goes to work tired every morning, with a feeling of doom that clings to her like staticky clothes.

On the first Thursday in November, Ollie LaChance pats Ara on the back with great affection. 'Well done, Arabella. I'm proud of you. It's your best work yet.' He hands her the issue of *Le Ti-Cajun Gazette* with Hooty's picture on the cover. The headline reads: Hooty Birmingham – Home is where the sax is …

'It made the cover?'

'Good work, kiddo. There's great passion in your writing.'

'It's not passion. I'm not a passionate person. Haven't got a passionate bone in this body.'

'Why so defensive?' Ollie says. 'It's a compliment. Let me take you to the Bayou for a burger.'

Ollie orders them a couple of bacon burgers with extra cheddar and raw onions and a side order of spiced fries. 'It's okay to splurge,' he says. 'Everyone needs a thick burger once in a while.'

'Tell that to my butt.'

Ollie reaches for her hand. 'I feel like you're my prodigy,' he says proudly. 'You're my very own Eliza Doolittle. From housewife to star reporter under the tutelage of Oliver LaChance.'

Ara blushes.

'You surprise me,' he continues. 'At first I thought you were simply beautiful. Now I know you're so much more.' He squeezes her hand. 'Are you sure there can't be something more between us?'

Ara snatches her hand away. 'There's someone else,' she says.

Ollie's face falls. 'Who? What does he have that I don't?'

'Never mind who, Oliver, you're my boss. Anything more than a platonic relationship would be inappropriate.'

The burgers and fries land on the table in front of them with a thud. The waitress, a gum-chewing redhead, winks in Ollie's direction. 'Enjoy,' she says coyly, and saunters away with her hips swaying like a palm tree in a storm.

'Did she wink at me?' he asks.

Ara nods. 'She was flirting.'

They bite into their burgers, letting the red juice squirt and dribble down their chins. Ara does love a good bacon-burger every once in a while. Now that it's just her and Kenny, she doesn't often get the opportunity.

Back at the office, Ara finds a message Scotch-taped to her phone. Call your mother ASAP.

'Mama?' Ara bellows, her heart thumping in her chest. 'What's the matter? Is Kenny okay?'

Melva blows her nose into the phone. 'It's Nectar,' she whimpers. 'He's taken a turn for the worse.'

'You're not crying, are you?' Ara says suspiciously.

'He's my husband. Of course I'm a little sad.'

'Oh, please.'

'Listen, he's in the hospital. He doesn't have much longer.'

The walls of the Lafayette Parish Hospital are painted the faintest banana yellow, an improvement over the Crest-blue walls in Montréal.

'Two hospitals in two weeks,' Kenny says, staring out the window at the parking lot.

'This must be hard for you,' Nectar says in a gruff voice. They can hear the mucus in his throat. He is hooked up to more wires than a TV set and is withering to nothingness right in front of them. It's hard for Kenny to look. Mostly he hovers around the window, staring out at the cars in the lot. Nectar is essentially a corpse, breathing only because of a respirator.

Melva sits at his side, pretending to be distraught and dabbing melodramatically at her eyes with a tissue. Ara is worried about Kenny, about the damage two back-to-back tragedies will have on him. First his real father, now his substitute father. It's too much suffering in too short a time for a sensitive twelve-year-old boy.

'Melva, you finally got your wish,' Nectar sputters. 'I'm almost dead.'

'You were a good husband,' she sobs. 'I never really meant anything I said.'

Nectar rolls his eyes. 'This performance is worthy of a Golden Globe.'

Melva sneers. 'Shut up.'

Nectar coughs so hard it's like he could cough himself to death. Kenny flinches, blocks his ears.

'I don't have much time . . .' Nectar rasps.

'Shh.' Ara pats his leg affectionately.

'Will you deliver the last of my crocheted sweaters to the Clothes Horse?'

'Of course.'

'And keep one for yourself,' he tells Ara, exploding into a fit of coughing that makes them all squirm. He is inches away from the end of his life, they all know it. It hangs in the air ominously, like his flatulence.

'We should go,' Ara says. Nectar could die at any second and she doesn't want Kenny to be a witness. 'We'll be back tomorrow.'

Nectar smiles faintly. He appreciates Ara's politeness.

'You've been a good friend, Kenny,' he says. 'Thanks for keeping me company these last weeks.'

Kenny nods and shuffles out of the room. Ara leans forward and pecks Nectar's forehead. The smell of death seeps out of his pores. 'You've been good to me,' she says.

'Take care of yourself,' he whispers into Ara's ear. 'You're like a flower that somehow managed to bloom in a wasteland.'

She squeezes his bony hand, brushes a tear from her cheek and joins Kenny in the banana-yellow corridor. Nectar Spurnicky passes on three hours later, with Melva by his side, breathing a sigh of relief.

The reading of his will is a ceremonious little gathering which immediately precedes the funeral. Melva is positively glowing as Nectar's lawyer opens his briefcase and pulls out the documentation. She is grinning from ear to ear, right up until the will is read out loud, at which point that wide grin freezes on her face in horror. Nectar bequeathed his entire fortune to Kenny, to be administered by Arabella until Kenny's eighteenth birthday. To Melva, his beloved wife, Nectar left the modest profits from his crocheted sweaters – a grand total of $6,500 – and their house.

The next morning Melva puts her house up for sale. 'You two better be prepared to move out as soon as this house is sold,' she tells Ara. Then she mutters, 'I ought to go an' spit on that man's grave.'

Melva's relationship with Kenny, despite his being her grandson, is now virtually terminated. The inheritance causes a permanent rift between them which doesn't seem to bother Kenny in the least, although it does sadden Ara.

Arabella and Kenny move out shortly thereafter. They rent a lovely condo on Butcher Switch Road and decorate it in shades of lavender and kelly green. They buy antiques in St Martinville Parish and order furniture from the Pottery Barn. Ara buys plants and floral throw cushions, cast iron candelabras and Gustav Klimt reproductions. Together they turn the condo into a home and start all over.

* * *

PERFECTING HER CHARACTER

Icons and Illusions, Part I

By Dayna Slominski – Special to *Hot off the Press!*

What is it about fame that so intrigues us? We send out the paparazzi to capture our icons at play and to record their every private moment. We hungrily invade their lives, as though our own are too empty. We scream when we see them in person and we cherish their hastily scrawled signatures on napkins. We claw at their 'perfect,' shiny lives like hungry cats. We are insatiable when it comes to fame.

And who isn't blinded by the sheen? Who doesn't secretly, diligently count every pound Oprah sheds or puts on?

We must begin to examine at what point our icons become illusions. Is it the illusion that draws us in, or the possibility that beneath all that glitter, glamour and perfection there lurks a real person with morning breath and menstrual cramps like the rest of us?

Here's a news flash: Movie stars are mere mortals, no matter how rich, famous and beautiful they are. However, in our society those very qualities elevate a human being to mythic proportions. Talent be damned – it's not a requirement. But how many magazine covers you get on is.

Fame is a window into the lives of people whom we perceive as better than us, luckier than us, more gifted than us. These days we want more details, more illicit photographs, more gossip – and the nastier the better. And while it's fun to live vicariously through the Madonnas and Oprahs of the world, it's even more fun to watch them topple from their precarious pedestals.

And inevitably they do. They screw up, they make bad movies, they gain weight, they age. And therein lies the secret of our obsessions: the unravelling of the icon, the shattering of the illusion. That moment when we watch another person – someone who has attained all the things we have only ever dreamed about – come crashing down in front of the entire world, is the precise moment our own unspectacular lives become validated.

And then we don't feel so bad. Then we are thankful that it isn't our own six-week stint in rehab on the cover of the *Enquirer*.

Ara glues the article onto the first page of a scrapbook she bought at Pharmax, then writes DAYNA'S CAREER in black marker on the cover. She tucks the scrapbook into her underwear drawer and smiles proudly to herself.

In the days that follow, Ara goes through the motions of her life with only mild enthusiasm: she drops Kenny off at school, edits lamentable stories on French Louisiana, ducks Oliver's frequent and persistent advances, cooks unremarkable vegetarian suppers for herself and Kenny, watches an hour of sitcoms while Kenny reads in his bedroom, tucks him in at nine and then stays up watching late-night TV until she falls asleep.

There is the nagging feeling that something vital is missing from her routine. She suspects it has to do with Hooty. He's left a gap inside her which nothing seems to fill.

Gypsi disagrees. She says, 'If you're feeling empty and purposeless, it's because you are empty and purposeless.'

'Thanks.'

Gypsi butters a steaming honey bran muffin and hands it to Ara on a tea saucer. Ara accepts it gratefully. 'All's I'm saying,' Gypsi continues, 'is you can't blame the emptiness on a man. No man should be expected to fill you up.'

'I'm not a gas tank.'

'Yes, you are. And you're empty. It's time to stop looking to Hooty to replenish you. If something is missing, it's missing from *within you*.'

The muffin melts in Ara's mouth, slides smoothly down her throat. 'There's nothing wrong with a man making a woman feel whole,' she says.

'Of course there is,' Gypsi argues. 'Ask yourself this, Ara. Why don't you feel whole on your own?'

'Because I miss Hooty.'

Gypsi rolls her eyes. 'You can't expect a man to salvage you, Arabella. He should complement you, not resuscitate you.'

'Maybe I want to be resuscitated. I'm so bored these days, just flailing around my life like a fish on sand.'

'It's because you're cut off from your spirit. A woman needs spirituality in her life.'

'Where can I get some?' Ara asks impatiently. 'I've wanted some for a while now.'

'Inside yourself, hon.'

'Come on, Gyps. Give me a tangible answer. Something I can work with.'

'All right. There's meditation, yoga, martial arts. I studied karate for years in New York. I'm a green belt. It's very spiritual and also you learn how to kick men in the groin.'

'My bum will look awful in those white pyjamas,' Ara says. 'Do you think it can actually help?'

'I know it can. Plus those karate guys are real flexible if you know what I mean.' She winks, then jabs Ara in the ribs with her elbow. 'Nothing wrong with indulging in a healthy sexual fantasy while you're getting in touch with your spiritual side.'

Later, Ara walks the four blocks to the Lafayette Karate Dojo and signs up for a white belt karate class with Sensei Henry. The walls are lined with posters of him in different karate poses or draped in an assortment of impressive belts. The entire school is something of a shrine to him. Ara fills out a long form, answering questions about her weight and why she wants to learn karate, and then she pays six hundred dollars to join the orange belt program.

Sensei Henry is short, Caucasian and built like a refrigerator. His arms are sprinkled with orange freckles and gold hair. He says by way of introduction: 'I am Sensei Henry. I am a white man and I was born in Kentucky, but I have been to Okinawa. As the founder of modern karate, Gichin Funakoshi, once said, the art of karate lies not in victory or defeat but in the perfection of the character of its participants. Now gimme fifty jumping jacks following my count.'

After a lengthy warm-up in which Ara realizes she is grossly out of shape and embarrassingly inflexible, Sensei Henry sends her off into a corner to learn the *tewaza* with Sensei Bucky – also Caucasian and built like a refrigerator but with pubescent acne and braces on his teeth.

'Ready position,' he says, bending his legs and holding his right fist in front of his face. Ara copies him and tries to follow him through a series of confusing arm movements. 'One, two, three ...'

Ara messes up on the fourth move over and over again. 'I don't see how this is going to help me defend myself,' she snaps. 'All these stupid dance moves. Isn't the purpose of this to hurt somebody?'

Sensei Bucky slaps his chest with two balled fists. 'These are blocks,' he says impatiently. 'Blocks are one of the most important techniques in karate. You have to learn them first.'

Ara sighs. 'If I was in danger,' she says, 'I don't think these little face block thingies would help me.'

Sensei Bucky stares at her with a blank, pimply face. 'The *kumite* comes later,' he says.

'What's *kumite*?'

'It is sparring. The physical confrontation.'

'Like fighting?'

'Yes, fighting.'

'Well, I'd like to skip right to the inflicting-pain techniques,' she asks. 'Or the spiritual stuff.'

'You have to learn the *tewaza* first,' he says impatiently, and then in a firmer voice, 'Ready position!'

Ara limps home miserably after the class. *Spirituality, my ass*, she thinks. All she's got to show for that hour of karate is a sore back. The pain intensifies all the way home. She has a hot bath and gets straight into bed but it still feels like someone is jabbing a hockey stick into her lower back. Kenny comes up at suppertime and says, 'Mom, I'm hungry now.'

'I can't walk,' she tells him.

'How come?'

'I threw my back out looking for spirituality.'

'Does that mean no stir-fry?'

'Why don't you order a pizza, slugger? I'm incapacitated for the night.'

'Pizza's too greasy,' he says. 'I'll get pimples.'

'Kenny, eat what you want. And get me a pain killer from the medicine cabinet.'

Kenny, not used to such harsh words coming from his mother, scurries obediently to the bathroom. He tends to himself all night, even tucks himself into bed.

Ara dreams Sensei Henry is giving her a lethal *shuto* strike to the lower back. She wakes up screaming, unable to sit up. She tries to slither out of bed but crumples to the floor, her legs like two broken matchsticks. She lies there prostrate on the floor for an hour or so, until Kenny comes in around eight that morning.

'Why didn't you wake me for school?' he asks her.

'I can't move,' she tells him.

'Why are you on the floor?'

'I fell down.'

He kneels beside her and helps her back into bed.

'The ceiling needs painting,' she comments.

She is immobile for the next four days. She uses the free time to daydream about Hooty and imagine herself back in New Orleans, reunited with him at the Maison Dupuis. He sent her a postcard from Beale Street in Memphis, but that was a long time ago – somewhere between Roman's coma and Nectar's death. There hasn't been much time to write back, besides which, there was no return address on the postcard.

Imagine, she has fallen in love with a jazz nomad.

Gypsi drops by during the week and leaves Ara a phone number of a masseuse in Cecilia. When Ara is able to hobble about with the help of an old crutch Gypsi dug up in her tool shed, she takes a cab to Cecilia for an appointment with Krista Potemkin. Miss Potemkin, a fortyish Russian emigré with dyed red hair and lots of clanking jewellery, has her studio on the top floor of a Laundromat. The sign on her door says: Masseuse/Psychotherapist.

Ara knocks, leaning heavily on her crutch. 'Enter, enter,' says Krista Potemkin, her bracelets and earrings jingling. The room is small and overwhelmingly red. A gel on the only lamp casts a red glow so that there is the feeling of being in a darkroom. There are candles burning all over the room and shelves lined with bottles of herbs and spices. Ara lies belly-down on a cot. The room smells of rose sachets.

'Vhere is your pain?' Miss Potemkin says, rubbing massage oil into the palms of her hands.

'My lower back.'

'The back is like luggage for stress, you know.' She rolls her r's, sounds like Natasha from 'Rocky and Bullwinkle'. 'Vhen vee are stressed, vee carry it in the back.'

'I pulled it doing karate. I'm in deplorable shape. I don't think it's stress.'

Miss Potemkin laughs. 'It's alvays stress. Now remove your clothes,' she says.

Ara does so reluctantly. 'I know I need to lose a few pounds,' she admits, lifting her shirt over her head.

'I am not concerned vith the outer flesh,' she says. 'I only care about the flesh of the mind. Vhen the mind is tense, the muscles are tense.'

She begins to work her fingers into Ara's back, starting at the neck and moving slowly downward. 'Your body is like a plank of vood, voman.'

'I'm sorry,' Ara mutters.

'Your soul must be tortured, poor creature. Your thoughts in knots!'

Miss Potemkin continues to massage Ara's back with her knuckles and then the palms of her hands. Ara feels like a lump of pizza dough, being kneaded this way and that.

'I notice you're also a psychotherapist,' Ara mumbles, her mouth pressed against the cot.

'In Volgograd, yes. I vas a practicing therapist. Here in America, my licence is no good. I became a masseuse to make the ends meet. But let me tell you something: you can take the voman out of psychotherapy but you cannot take the psychotherapist out of the voman.'

'Can you really cure people with talk?' Ara asks her.

'Cure, no. Heal, yes.' Miss Potemkin squirts oil onto Ara's back. Ara squeals. 'This is vhere it hurts?' she asks, digging her knuckle into Ara's lower back.

'Ouch. Yes.'

'Your muscles are locked, and do you know vhere the key is?'

Ara shakes her head.

'In here, Ms Boot.' She taps Ara on the side of her head. 'You must relax your mind as vell as your body. Vhat is the true source of your pain?'

Ara thinks about it, then shrugs. 'I'm lonely?' she says, phrasing it as a question.

'Forget the present,' she says, slapping Ara's back like she's playing the bongos. 'Go into the past and delve into the svimming pool that is your pain. Delve delve delve!'

Ara concentrates, imagining an Olympic-size swimming pool full of crystal-blue pain. She sees herself holding her breath, diving in and breast-stroking her way to the ledge. Miss Potemkin's words reverberate in her thoughts: *Delve delve delve*. She is vaguely conscious of Miss Potemkin's fingers working the muscles of her back; the cling-clang of her jewellery; the smell of roses in her own nostrils.

Then Miss Potemkin climbs onto the cot and cracks Ara's back with a forceful jab of her knee. 'Now come up for breath and tell me vhat you see!' she cries.

Ara opens her eyes. She sees Melva.

The next day is Sunday, cold with a flat cloudless sky. Ara rises easily from her bed, is able to walk from her bedroom down to the kitchen without the crutch. She peers through her kitchen window onto the street, checking for signs of snowflakes or nuggets of hail. It's that sort of day.

She notices a blue Oldsmobile parked across the street but thinks nothing of it. Then she remembers it's Remembrance Day and makes a mental note to respect a minute of silence at eleven. Kenny joins her for a breakfast of blueberry pancakes with dollops of sour cream – a Sunday favourite.

'These are swell,' Kenny says. Ara looks up from her Jumble and touches his chin affectionately. 'Better than IHOP,' he adds.

'That's a compliment.'

'It's because you use fresh frozen blueberries. IHOP uses blueberry syrup.'

'It's all in the fresh frozen blueberries.'

Kenny puts his fork down then and stares up into her face as though trying to assess something in her features.

'What is it?' she asks him.

'I have something to tell you.'

'What is it, son? Trouble at school?'

Kenny shakes his head and averts his eyes from her face. He squishes a blueberry with his finger. 'I have a date,' he announces solemnly.

'A date?' Ara gasps. 'With a girl?'

'With Rosemary Moncoeur. She's in my class.'

'A date?' Ara sputters. 'But you're only twelve.'

'Rosemary shaves,' he informs her proudly.

Ara bites her knuckle and looks down helplessly at the newspaper in front of her. 'A date,' she breathes.

'She invited me to Mongo Gruber's birthday. It's a couples party.'

'A couples party?' Ara cries. He might as well have said orgy. 'And you want to go? Because if you don't, I'll call this Rosemary girl and tell her you can't.'

'Oh no, Mom, I want to go.'

'So –'

'So, I guess I'm not queer,' he says.

And as if the little angel of Machismo had personally whispered news of Kenny's heterosexuality into Roman Boot's ear, Roman's eyes fluttered open that very afternoon. According to the nurse he just woke up as though from a nap. But he didn't say anything and his eyes were flat; he just lay there staring up at the ceiling. The nurse said the brain damage might be permanent but it was too soon to tell. 'He may live the rest of his life as a vegetable,' she announced dramatically.

'Which one?' Ara asked in an ill-timed attempt at humour. The nurse was not amused but Ara, imagining Roman as an asparagus stalk, chuckled softly.

Ara tells Kenny about Roman's current state as delicately as the situation will allow. 'Your father's out of the coma,' she says hesitantly.

'Is he back to normal?'

'Not exactly, pal. He may have brain damage.'

'Damage how?'

'He could be like a child forever,' she explains. 'Totally helpless.'

'A child?' Kenny breathes. 'Poor Dad.'

'It's okay to cry,' Ara soothes. 'It's healthy.'

'I don't feel any tears,' he confesses, his head hanging low.

'That's understandable, Kenny. Your father is still alive. At least you have that to be thankful for.'

'I want to visit Dad at Christmas,' he says.

Ara tousles his hair. 'Of course we will, slugger.'

Still the promise does not bring a smile to his lips. He stares straight ahead without saying another word, his brows converging in concentration. His strength is admirable but Ara still worries about the scars she can't see. It won't be much longer before he is skidding through his teen years, pushing her away as most boys do. Without a father figure to guide him, who knows which way he'll stray? She wants to wrap her arms around him and squeeze all his pain away. She wants to save him from angst and suffering and the ravages of puberty. She'd like to keep him just as he is, on the cusp of adolescence with all his innocence intact. If only you could preserve such things in formaldehyde, she thinks.

The worry lines in his forehead are premature. He is growing up.

She takes him to the Dairy Queen near his school in an effort to cheer him up. Ice cream has been known to console both Kenny and

Dayna in the past; perhaps the circumstances were less dire, but one must never underestimate the powers of a caramel sundae.

En route, Ara glances into her rearview mirror and spots the blue Oldsmobile that was parked outside her house that morning. The Oldsmobile follows her along Johnston, staying two cars behind.

'What is it, Mom? Why do you keep looking behind?'

'No reason,' Ara says, preoccupied. 'What size sundae do you want?'

Poetry

'CLOSE THE BLIND and sit down,' Gypsi says.

Ara is peering out the window. 'I'm sure I saw him on my way over. He was turning the corner as I snuck out the back door.'

'You're getting paranoid.'

'I'm being *stalked*.'

'It's only been three days.'

Ara is spotting the blue Oldsmobile all over the place now; on her way to work, outside the *Gazette* office by the KOA campground, in front of her condo. Monday morning it tailed her all the way to Kenny's school.

At first she brushed it off, dismissed it as creative melodrama or her imagination in overdrive. Who on earth would stalk *her*? But there is the overriding feeling of being observed, spied on. Ara snaps the blind shut and drops into a chair.

For once Gypsi's kitchen doesn't smell of fresh-baked pies or muffins or tarts. It smells of Mr Clean. Ara is disappointed. 'Anyhow,' she says. 'I came for a palm reading. I'm at a crossroads and to tell you the truth I'm depressed.'

'Join the club,' Gypsi mutters.

'Oh, Gyps, I don't mean to impose. I can come back tomorrow.'

'I can't read your palm today or tomorrow or maybe ever,' Gypsi says bleakly.

'What's wrong?'

'I'm blocked. I've been slipping lately and it started when I failed to predict the fortune you recently inherited. I think I've lost my gift somewhere along the way.'

'Maybe I just have bad palms,' Ara suggests.

Gypsi shakes her head. 'There's no such thing as bad palms, only bad palm readers.'

Ara pats Gypsi's hand reassuringly and says, 'I'm sure your gift will come back.'

Gypsi frowns. 'I think it's the change.'

'What change?'

Gypsi leans forward. 'Menopause,' she whispers. 'Menopause has skewed my psychic gift.'

'I had no idea.'

Gypsi nods solemnly. 'My hormones are in an upheaval. The entire balance of my biological system is out of sync. My psychic power is just one casualty.'

'I don't know what to say.'

'Can I offer you a cup of Swiss-almond-flavoured coffee with a dash of Irish Cream?'

'No thanks. Flavoured coffee makes my glands swell.'

'Anyhow, my low spirits are hormonal,' Gypsi explains.

'Mine are maternal,' Ara says. 'I'm afraid I've damaged Kenny permanently with my selfishness and my voodoo doll.'

'How so?'

'First off, I plucked him out of his comfortable life back home and dragged him here to Lafayette to begin a new life without even consulting him. Then I put his father in a coma –'

'*Tanya* put Roman in a coma.'

'But I'm indirectly responsible,' Ara whines. 'Besides, the end result is that Kenny has a vegetable for a father. And then Nectar passed away –'

'That wasn't your fault.'

'No, but I was so preoccupied with Hooty I never even noticed that Mama was pouring Liquid Plumm'r in Nectar's eggshakes.'

'Huh?'

'That's not to say the Liquid Plumm'r killed him. The throat cancer would have got him anyway, but who knows? Maybe I'm partly responsible for speeding up his demise and henceforth depriving Kenny of a dear friend.' She pauses for a breath and then, 'Maybe I'll have just a dash of that Irish Cream, hold the coffee.'

Gypsi retrieves a bottle of Bailey's from her pantry and pours a shot into a coffee mug.

'The worst part is,' Ara continues, 'Kenny has a date.'

'What's so terrible about that?'

'Gypsi, the boy is only twelve and already he's turning to the flesh of a woman for solace. Just a month ago he wouldn't have been able to pick a girl out of a line-up. Now I've pushed him into the arms of a tramp. And she shaves!'

'It's just a date.'

'He's growing up, Gyps, and I just wasn't prepared.' Ara dumps the shot down her throat. 'I know it sounds terrible,' she says, 'but I'm more worried about Kenny's first date than I am about the thug in the blue Oldsmobile. I think I can better handle the thug.'

Gypsi gently pats Ara's shoulder. 'I'm not a parent. I don't know what to say.'

'Maybe I should move back to Montréal so Kenny can be closer to Roman. Besides, it's safer.'

'Safer how? You don't think there are twelve-year-old girls who shave in Montréal?'

'Then how can I protect Kenny?'

'Do you mean how can you keep him a child?'

Ara shrugs. 'Maybe.'

'You can't. Not here and not in Montréal. But Ara, you can't blame yourself for the natural passage of time. You have to accept the changes. You might be sad about it for a while, but you'll adjust.'

Ara helps herself to another shot of Irish Cream. 'I wish I could see the future.'

'So do I.'

They hold hands at the table, as though to generate strength between them. Perhaps joined together they can bide time and hold the unfamiliar at bay.

With a sudden burst of energy, Gypsi jumps up from the table and clasps her hands together. 'I have a temporary solution to our woes.'

'What's that?'

'A ride on my old man's Harley. It's poetry in motion, hon.'

Ara, not sure how a ride on the back of a motorcycle can soothe her fears and anxieties, reluctantly lets Gypsi guide her out to the garage. 'Isn't he gorgeous?' Gypsi says, stroking the bike's leather seat and shiny chrome body.

'How can this help me?' Ara wants to know. 'I'm afraid of

motorcycles. And the blue Oldsmobile is sure to follow us.'

'Trust me,' Gypsi says. 'It'll be uplifting.' She hands Ara a black helmet with the words 'Biker Chick' printed across the front and a black leather jacket. 'You'll need this. It'll be cold out there.'

'What if we're followed?' Ara asks, zipping up the jacket and then pulling the helmet over her head.

'Then we'll ask whoever it is in that Oldsmobile what the hell he wants.' Gypsi throws her leg over the Harley as though she's mounting a horse. 'Get on and hold tight!' she cries.

'Where do I hold on?'

'My waist, hon.'

'Is there a seat belt? Something to keep me safe?'

'You'll be safe,' Gypsi promises.

'Is there a foot rest? My legs are just dangling here.'

'Relax, sister. Enjoy the ride!' With that she roars out of the garage and onto Boudreaux Avenue with Ara yelping like a terrified puppy behind her.

'Slow down! Slow down!' Ara shrieks, but her voice is drowned out by the motor. When Gypsi comes to a stop at a red light, Ara leans forward and shouts into her ear, 'What's to keep us from tipping over?'

'Speed, honey! Speed!' And off they go. Ara closes her eyes and concentrates on a series of intricate breathing techniques which have helped her to relax in the past. Aside from the fear of smashing head on into the back of a Mack truck or of being hurled over the handle bars and landing upside down on her cranium, there is something to be said for the wind whipping her face and the freedom it inspires. She smiles despite her determination not to enjoy herself. 'Where are we going?' she bellows into Gypsi's ear.

'Destination is not the point!' Gypsi says. 'Just enjoy the ride!'

'Okay!'

And then it occurs to her: *this is it. This* is freedom. It's emancipation. Two women on a Harley flying across a highway with the wind stinging their eyes and nothing but luck between them and the pavement.

'I've been emancipated!' Arabella screams.

'You're constipated?' Gypsi says.

'*Emancipated!* I had an epiphany, Gyps!'

'There's Tums in my bag. Hold on a bit, okay?'

'I said e-man-ci-pated!' But the words are carried off by the wind. No matter. The moment does not have to be pared down to a sentence and verbalized to be meaningful. Her whole body is swollen with the moment, and that's enough.

Somewhere along the Evangeline Thruway, just as her muscles are starting to relax and her heartbeat has returned to its regular pace, Ara looks behind her and notices the navy blue Oldsmobile three cars behind, swerving in and out of traffic to keep up with them. Something like a dead weight lands with a thud in the pit of her stomach. She gets the urge to lean over the Harley and vomit. 'Gypsi!' she wails. 'We're being followed!'

Gypsi glances into the rearview mirror. Without warning she veers into the far left lane towards Opelousas. 'We've got to get off the thruway!' Ara says.

Gypsi nods and jerks the bike in the direction of the Bernard Street exit. Ara twists around to check for the Oldsmobile, which is keeping pace with them easily. 'We've got to go faster!'

Gypsi accelerates, taking Church Street straight to North University Avenue. 'Do you have any idea where we're headed?' Ara wants to know.

'North!' Gypsi says.

Ara looks behind her, devastated to see the Oldsmobile still on her tail. 'Do something!' she pleads. Gypsi doesn't give the matter much thought. She cranks the gas with two lethal flicks of her wrist and makes a sharp left turn into the Bayou Wilderness RV Resort. The Harley skids dangerously in the dirt, but Gypsi manages to keep it upright. She eases up on the gas and comes to a full stop between two massive RVs.

'Did we ditch him?' she asks, pulling off her helmet.

Ara slides off the bike and looks around. The entrance to the grounds is empty. There is no sign of the Oldsmobile, not even the sound of an engine running in the distance. Ara and Gypsi stare at each other expectantly. Ara removes her helmet and shakes her hair out. 'I think we did it.'

Gypsi squeals. 'Yee-haaaw!'

'Wow.'

'YEEHAW!'

'Oh boy,' Ara breathes. 'That was fantastic!' Ara's heart is slapping loudly against her chest. She takes a deep breath, wipes the perspiration from her neck and forehead. 'We really lost him.'

'Holy Hell's Angels!' Gypsi whoops. 'What a ride!'

'Now what?'

Gypsi looks around. 'How about lunch? The cafeteria overlooks the bayou.'

Ara nods. 'A car chase does leave one rather hungry.'

'Afterward I'll challenge you to a game of shuffleboard.'

Ara and Gypsi hobble off to the resort's cafeteria. 'My bum hurts,' Ara complains.

'You get used to it.'

Ara is so inspired by her first ride on the back of a motorcycle she writes a poem later on by the pool.

She calls it 'Hog Wild'.

'I didn't know you were a poet,' Gypsi says, skimming a polished toe along the surface of the freezing water.

'Neither did I. But there are … *things* lurking inside me I never knew about. Passions.'

'It happens at forty. "Things" start to come up.'

'Does it happen to all women, Gyps?'

'To the lucky ones. There has to be a foundation there for it.'

'A foundation of what?'

'Oh, a bunch of different things. Strength and courage. And luck, of course.'

'It feels, well, mystical,' Ara confides, wrapping her arms around her body to keep warm. 'Like I'm being rearranged inside. Reorganized.'

'I call it the shift.'

'Like the change?'

'Oh no, nothing like that. The shift isn't hormonal. It has to do with priorities.'

'How so?' she asks Gypsi. The chlorine smell, as always, is

comforting. Ara thinks of Dayna's childhood, her own childhood.

'You stop living for others is all,' says Gypsi. 'You stop trying to please people all the time and you start pleasing yourself for a change. You take what you want: the white meat off the chicken, the biggest piece of pie.'

'Gypsi, I envy you. You're such a feminist.'

'If that's what you call a woman who knows and says the truth, then so be it.'

'Isn't it selfish, this shift? I do have children,' Ara reminds her.

'What's wrong with selfish?' Gypsi says. 'Don't be afraid of being selfish. Your children are part of your Self. Your maternal priorities will never change.'

'How do you know so much, Gypsi?'

'I read books, honey. And I observe.'

'You listen, too.'

'There's that,' she says. 'How about a frozen yogurt?'

'Strawberry,' Ara says. 'Large.'

She watches Gypsi disappear behind an RV. There is still such a long way to go, she thinks tiredly. But then there is also a ripple of optimism.

Kumite

TANYA CALLS at the very end of November to tell Ara the big news: she was found not guilty of attempted murder in the second degree. She *was* found guilty of assault causing bodily harm, a crime punishable by up to fourteen years in prison, but the sentence was commuted to 140 hours of community service. 'It was a crime of passion,' she explains. 'The jury understood that Roman's actions were actually the cause of this whole mess. Just like the Bobbitt trial. That was a crime of passion, too. He cheated on her so she chopped his thing off. Roman cheated on me so I bopped him on the head a few times. And now I've been vindicated. I've decided to devote the rest of my life to caring for him.'

'Who, Roman?'

'Of course Roman. I'll be moving into your house. He needs round-the-clock care.'

'How does Roman feel about that?'

Tanya laughs. 'Who knows? He can't speak! Anyhow, I'm redoing the bedroom. I find that shade of peach you chose so eighties. I'm repainting everything sage.'

'Sage?'

'Mmm. It's marvellous. Very nineties.'

'It won't be easy, you know, caring for a vegetable.'

'It's not for sure there's permanent brain damage. Anyway, this is a labour of love. I *love* that vegetable.'

'I hope you'll be happy then,' Ara offers insincerely.

'I'd like to bury the hatchet if it's possible. I mean, a jury found me not guilty, I don't see why you shouldn't.'

'The jury didn't catch you having sex with him.'

'You always have a witty retort,' Tanya says.

'I do?' Ara takes this as something of a compliment. She has never viewed herself as a witty person. 'Thank you.'

'It wasn't a compliment,' Tanya snaps. 'You know, you've changed a lot, Arabella.'

'I have?'

'You hardly seem like the same person. You've lost something – that quality that made you so endearing and soft.'

'I'm still soft.'

Tanya snorts indignantly. 'You're just not the same.'

'I may have a thicker shell but I'm still soft on the inside.'

'Men don't like women with hard exteriors. It's off-putting.'

'I have a lot more important things to worry about,' Ara says. 'If you must know, I'm being followed.'

'By who?'

'If I knew, I wouldn't be so damn scared.'

'Maybe it's the mob,' Tanya says.

'The mob? Why on earth –'

'Wasn't your father blown up by the Mafia?'

'Yes, he was, but he was just in the wrong place at the wrong time. Certainly *I* have nothing to do with it.'

'Maybe I shouldn't be talking to you,' Tanya says nervously. 'You know how they work, those people. Those mafiosos. One day I wind up dead in a garbage dumpster in a back alley. Why? Because I was talking to you! That's how they work, those people. Guilt by association. They don't need any more reason than that. So good luck then and I'll call you.'

The line goes dead in Ara's ear. She shivers.

Ara rings the doorbell twice but no one answers. She decides to let herself in with her key and leave a note. She finds Melva on her hands and knees on the kitchen floor, surrounded by cardboard boxes. There is a roll of masking tape hanging from her mouth.

Melva looks up, startled, as Ara comes into the kitchen. 'You didn't answer the door,' Ara says.

'I'm busy. How'd you get in?'

'I still have a key.'

'You scared me.'

'Sorry,' Ara mutters. 'Hi, Mama.'

Melva takes the tape out of her mouth. 'What are you doing here?'

'Just visiting.'

'I don't have time for a long visit,' Melva says. 'I sold the house and I'm moving to Miami.'

'Miami?'

'I'm gonna buy a condo or something with palm trees in the back yard and a pool and maybe a golf course. No more Cajun crapola.'

'You don't play golf.'

'That's irrelevant,' she says, dumping the contents of her junk drawer into a box. She writes JUNK in black marker. 'I need a change. I'm sick of swamps and bayous.'

'You could've told me.'

'I just did. Now either help me pack up some of these boxes or leave me alone to finish up.'

Ara kneels down and starts wrapping plates in old newspaper. 'Mama,' she says, 'I'm being followed.'

'Huh?'

'Someone's stalking me.'

'Who?'

'I have no idea. It's been three days now.'

'Maybe it's the mob,' Melva says.

'Mama! Why would you say that? Tanya said the same thing!'

'I'm just teasing. You're always so hysterical.'

But Ara's thoughts inevitably drift back to her childhood, to a time when Melva was always whispering the word *Mafia* as possible explanation for her husband's tragic death. The word was so ominous, could easily inspire terror in young Ara. She's always been jumpy at the sound of it, at the idea of Italian men with machine guns tucked into their dark suits. She used to worry about being blown up like her father wherever she went: at school, the movie theatre on Snowdon Street, summer camp. Who knew where the bomb would get her? She almost never ate pizza.

Time had ultimately quieted those fears and by the time of her first marriage, she rarely gave it much thought. Once she made the mistake of renting *The Godfather*, but she subsequently banned all movies starring Robert DeNiro and Joe Pesci.

'Mama, why was my daddy in New York anyway?' she asks.

Melva rips a piece of masking tape off the roll with her teeth and seals the junk box. 'He had some cousin in Brooklyn who had a lampshade business. Your dad wanted to get set up. If it worked out, he was gonna come back and get us. He got blown up on his first day.'

'You don't think his death is somehow connected to my being stalked?'

'Your father was a nobody, not worth the time it took to plant that damn bomb.'

'That's not a very nice thing to say.'

'You were better off growing up without him. He'd have made a lousy parent.'

'You were pretty lousy yourself.'

'Arabella Cusper!'

'It's the truth, Mama. The gloves are off. You were rotten.'

Melva slams her masking tape on the linoleum. 'Rotten?' she fires.

'That's what I said. I have a lot of pent-up rage, you know. I'm a swimming pool of pain inside.'

Melva stares at Ara, dumbfounded. 'A swimming pool of pain?'

'Yes. My therapist is helping me delve –'

'Your *who*?'

'My masseuse-slash-psychotherapist. She's been a tremendous help.'

'Another violin player, playing you for all you're worth.'

'Stop it.'

'Is that where all Nectar's dough is going? To a shrink?'

'*Masseuse*-slash-shrink.'

Melva shakes her head. 'There's not a scheme on earth you don't stumble into, not a scoundrel you don't fall prey to.'

'You being the worst scoundrel of them all.'

'Listen, Arabella, I know I'm not one of them gushy-pooh-pooh mothers, but I did my darnedest to raise you up good. This may be shocking because I'm not usually all gooey and sappy, but I ... you know ... do love you and stuff. What more can I give you, seeing as how *you* are the one with all of Nectar's money?'

'This has nothing to do with Nectar's money.'

'Oh, sure, you can afford to say that. You can afford not to have any financial woes.'

'Miss Potemkin was right,' Ara laments. 'You *are* the source of my emotional tension.'

Melva rolls her eyes. 'Well, I won't be causing you anymore *emotional tension* –' she spits out the words. 'I'm off to Miami next Monday. *For good.*'

'Old people live in Florida,' Ara says vindictively.

'Exactly,' Melva agrees. 'Which is why I'll be a pretty young thing compared to all those half-dead old ladies. I'll be sure to find a rich hubby, especially with these.' She shakes her breasts at Ara. 'The luscious breasts of a teenager!'

'Mama, this isn't what I wanted from you today.'

Melva lights a Winston. 'What did you want?'

Ara shrugs. 'Maybe an apology.'

'For what?'

'For who you are.'

'Ha! That'll be the day. I'm Melva Cusper an' proud of it. If you came here looking for someone else, too bad. This isn't the "Cosby Show".'

'I was here to give you another chance, Mama.'

'Then I guess I blew it,' she says indignantly. 'But let me tell you something, daughter. Why don't you ask that Miss Potemkin of yours about *acceptance*. You got me and you're stuck with me, and if you want to be happy in life you better learn to accept people as they are. I must have done something right, Arabella, because look how beautiful you turned out. And I don't just mean your large breasts.'

Ara swallows a lump in her throat. She stands up to leave.

'I'll send a postcard from Miami with my new address,' Melva says. 'You're welcome to come visit at Christmas. We can check out the young hunks at Daytona Beach.'

'I'll be visiting Roman in Montréal. He's out of the coma.'

'Any brain damage?'

'He's a vegetable.'

'He always was.'

'You really think I'm beautiful, Mama?'

Melva takes a long drag off her cigarette. 'You're no Candice Bergen but there's something about you.'

A Little Geisha

IN THE PARKING LOT of the Piggly Wiggly, Ara instinctively searches for the blue Oldsmobile. She counts four of them in all and curses herself for failing to check the licence plate of her stalker. She pushes a cart into the supermarket.

She dumps four quarts of lowfat milk into her cart and then manoeuvres herself towards the fruit and vegetable department. She tosses a bunch of bananas in and then quite suddenly stops. She looks around her dizzily. She closes her eyes and takes a long deep breath.

Now that the clouds of chaos have begun to part, a stream of sudden lucidity pours in like sunlight. Just like that, out of the blue and amidst all those bananas, it hits her. *I'm rich*. With all the fretting over Roman's coma, Nectar's death, the blue Oldsmobile and Kenny's date, there hasn't even been a minute to savour the fruits of her wealth. Oh, sure, the money legally belongs to Kenny and she wouldn't dream of abusing her privileges as his guardian, but gone is the burden of having to pay rent, put food on the table and put him through college. Besides, he has generously offered her a plump monthly allowance to do with whatever she pleases. He calls it her salary for being his mom.

'I'm rich,' she says aloud, half-stunned. *I didn't have to do anything, and I'm rich.*

She decides to prepare a festive celebration-dinner for Kenny: Cajun eggplant-zucchini Parmesan – his favourite and a welcome alternative to the monotony of stir-fry. As she reaches for the shiniest purple eggplant, she accidentally knocks down the strategically set-up pile which cascades to the floor in an eggplant avalanche. She gets down on her hands and knees and hurriedly tries to replace them before the supermarket display manager catches her.

'Let me give you a hand.'

Ara looks up. 'Oh, hi,' she says.

He smiles, starts picking up rolling eggplants. 'I haven't seen you in a while,' he says.

Ara shakes her head, chasing a stray eggplant. 'I hurt my back the very first day.'

Sensei Henry stands up with his thick arms full of eggplants, which look like grapes next to his gigantic bulging biceps. He's wearing his white karate pyjamas. 'So will you be back then, when your back is better?'

'I don't know. I was thinking of asking for a refund.'

'Ms Boot, I wouldn't have pegged you for a quitter.'

'I'm not a quitter, just uncoordinated.'

'Any determined person can master the art of karate. It requires nothing more than self-confidence and a strong will.'

Ara pushes her cart toward the zucchinis. Sensei Henry follows.

'I have a confession,' he says.

'Oh?'

'I followed you here today.'

'You what?'

'When you didn't come back to the dojo, I –'

'*You're* the blue Oldsmobile?'

Sensei Henry blushes and looks away. 'You noticed me.'

'Noticed?' Ara exclaims. 'I thought I was being stalked by the mob! I was about to contact the FBI.'

Sensei Henry chuckles. 'That's quite some imagination.'

'But *why*? Do you stalk all your customers when they skip a lesson?'

'Only the ravishing ones with twinkling eyes.'

Now Ara blushes.

'It was never my intention to frighten you,' he goes on. 'I only wanted to talk to you. That first day I came to your house I was going to invite you to a jujitsu tournament in Baton Rouge, but I just couldn't muster up the nerve to get out of my car.'

'Sensei –'

'Usually I'm a smooth operator with women,' he boasts. 'I have a gift. But with you, Ms Boot, well, your beauty renders me powerless. Your effervescent spirit reduces me to a spineless adolescent.'

'That's flattering, Mr Sensei, but –'

'Don't *but* me!' he cries. 'I've sat helplessly in my car watching you for days. I admit, my approach was questionable – it snowballed into something of an obsession. But now I've seized the perfect window of opportunity to express my feelings –'

'The produce section of the Piggly Wiggly?'

'Ms Boot, don't shun me. Have dinner with me tonight. I'll take you to the best sushi place in town.'

'I can't. I'm cooking Cajun eggplant-zucchini Parmesan for my son.'

'Tomorrow?'

'Do you always wear those pyjamas?'

'What about coffee?' he says desperately. 'Right now?'

Ara sighs. 'You shouldn't go around stalking women,' she tells him. 'It's creepy.'

'I'm a very intense man. I concede, I got carried away.'

'I wouldn't mind a cappuccino,' she says. 'But I have to finish my groceries first.'

'I'll accompany you.' He smiles broadly. Ara notices his front tooth is capped.

In the cereal aisle she throws a box of Sugaroos into the cart.

'Why not just inject poison directly into your bloodstream?' Sensei Henry remarks.

'I beg your pardon?'

'Sugaroos don't exactly contribute to a healthy mind and body, Ms Boot.'

'Kenny likes them.'

'Self-discipline must begin in the home.'

'I don't need a nutritionist,' Ara informs him tightly. Then she spitefully drops a box of Marshmallow Midgets into the cart.

'Feisty,' Sensei Henry says, peeling one of her bananas and biting into it. 'You can never have too much potassium.'

They go to EspressOh's! on Bertrand Street. Sensei Henry orders a decaf café au lait with nonfat milk. Ara has a cappuccino with caffeine, whole milk, a mountain of froth and chocolate sprinkles.

'So,' he says.

'So,' she says.

They are facing each other. Ara is thinking she doesn't like red-heads. She also doesn't like a stocky build or exaggerated muscles. Aside from the stalking, that's three more strikes against him.

'So,' Ara says again.

Sensei Henry is gazing at her with a vague expression on his face. The silence is torturous.

'What do you think of Rosie O'Donnell adopting a baby?' she asks him.

'Who?'

'She has a TV show.'

'I avoid entertainment,' he says. 'It weakens the spirit.'

'Tell that to my daughter.'

'Americans have no discipline,' he explains. 'That's the fundamental problem with this society. Discipline is the essence of martial arts.'

'How did you get involved with karate?'

'I was a child of five when Tsutomu Ohshima brought karate to America in 1955. I began my training three years later as a way to defend myself against grade school ruffians. But karate training soon teaches us that *real* strength comes from facing ourselves with severe eyes. Ohshima said that.'

Ara yawns.

'Karate originates in sixteenth-century Okinawa. Ever hear of *shaolin* boxing?'

'Uh, no.'

'Anyhoo, the key to karate is the ability to coordinate mind over body. A true karateist knows that he – or she – must be strong inwardly and gentle outwardly.'

'Mr Sensei, I don't like redheads.'

'Beg pardon?'

'It's no use. I'm hung up on Hooty.'

'Who?'

'Joe "Hooty" Birmingham.'

'The old jazz musician?'

'You've heard of him?'

'Sure.'

'Well, I love him. I'm not ready to date.'

'But he's a musician –'

'I know.'

'It's a dead end then,' he whimpers. 'I have so much to offer you, Arabella. Gishin Funokashi once –'

'Forget Funokashi! I – love – Hooty.'

'But you could be my little geisha.'

Ara, seething, stares at him across the table. Her eyes are flashing. 'Your little geisha?' she hisses. 'Do you think I left my husband, travelled 1,500 miles across the country, got robbed by a hitchhiker, put my ex in a coma, buried my stepfather and rode on the back of a Harley Davidson to wind up some karate nut's *little geisha*?' She slams her hand on the table. Sensei Henry's decaf spills over the side of his mug. 'I ought to pop you one,' she says.

'I'm a black belt in martial arts, Arabella!'

'Well, I'm a black belt in survival, buddy.'

The Great Gumbo

THE PHONE RINGS just as Ara is halfway out the door on her way to cover the grade two Cajun cook-off at Acadiana Primary. The cook-off is another of these small-town efforts to raise money for Les Amis de l'Immersion, a support group which helps keep the French immersion program alive in Louisiana elementary schools. Oliver is the sponsor of this event so first prize is dinner for two at the Bayou Bar and Grill and a full-page writeup in the *Cajun Gazette*.

Ara figures she's put on ten pounds since she started working for the paper. It seems the only way Louisianans know how to salvage their heritage is through food.

Ara dashes back to the phone. 'Hello?' she huffs, snatching up the receiver.

'Hel-lo.'

Ara gasps.

'Sur-prise,' he says.

'I thought –'

'It's a mir-a-cle.'

'Dear God,' Ara moans, slumping against the wall. 'They said the brain damage would probably be permanent.'

'I can't talk ver-y long,' Roman stammers. 'I'll lose my phone privi-leges.'

'But I thought you were back home,' Ara says.

'Tan-ya's rules –'

'She revokes your phone privileges?'

'She's strict.'

'We came to visit you in the hospital,' Ara tells him, checking her watch. She's late for the cook-off.

'When are you co-ming back to me?' he wants to know. His voice is thin and wavering.

'I'm not,' she says. 'Why would I?'

'You're my wife.'

'Not for much longer.'

'You'd di-vorce me af-ter what hap-pened to me?'

'I had nothing to do with it.'

'Still –'

'I'm happy here,' Ara says.

'But Ken-ny?'

'He's happy here, too.'

'You cold bitch.'

'Roman! How dare you just snap out of a damn coma without any permanent brain damage and then expect me to come running home to you! Besides, you're with Tanya now.'

'I have no choice. She won't leave.'

'Don't blame me for that.'

'Come home!'

'I will not.'

He starts to cry.

'Oh, stop it,' she says.

'Tan-ya's mean,' he whimpers.

'I'm not coming home.'

'Fine,' he wheezes. 'But you'll pay. This is not the last you'll hear of Ro-man ... what's my last name a-gain?'

'Boot.'

'Boot!' he cries. 'Ro-man Boot!'

She sighs and hangs up. She figured she was rid of him for good, without the hassle of a divorce. Now she'll have to look into a lawyer. *Darn darn darn.*

She locks the back door behind her, hops in her car and zooms off to the Acadiana Primary. That beautiful dream of a drooling, gurgling Roman has been shattered forever.

The Boob is back.

The banner out front says SAVE ARE HERITIGE. Ara winces. Kenny could spell 'our' correctly when he was in kindergarten. The education system in America is in decline, she thinks, climbing out of her car. She checks her purse for her notepad and tape recorder and disposable camera, then trots up the front steps to the school.

The principal greets her in the foyer. 'Ms Boot?' the woman says, holding out a long slender hand. 'I'm Mrs Bouvier, as in Jackie-O.'

Mrs Bouvier has a well-polished sheen; crisp silver hair, evenly pencilled lips, a good posture and sturdy handshake. Her teeth are pale yellow, but nothing a little Polident can't fix. She wears a classic smoke-grey blazer with matching flares.

Ara shakes her hand. 'I'm Arabella Slominski Boot, soon to be just Arabella once and for all.'

Mrs Bouvier's lip twitches like a bunny's nose. She says, 'I hope you're hungry,' and then leads Ara down the corridor towards the gym.

'How much are you hoping to raise?' Ara asks.

'Last year we raised four hundred dollars,' Mrs Bouvier says proudly.

Ara scribbles the number on her notepad. 'That's a lot of money for a trumped-up bake sale,' she remarks.

'This is a Cajun *cook-off*,' Mrs Bouvier spits. 'Our parents put a lot of effort into their dishes. In '84, one of our mothers won the Pillsbury Bake-Off with her Creole praline pie. She's here today with her million-dollar recipe.'

'I didn't –'

'And another of our fathers is the sous-chef at the Andouille Epicée on Vermilion. He makes a prize-winning gumbo, Mrs *Boot*. This isn't some amateur shindig, you know.'

'I didn't mean anything by it –'

'I'll just let the food do the rest of the talking,' Mrs Bouvier snips. 'Enjoy your afternoon.'

She click-clicks out of the gymnasium leaving Arabella in the lingering swirl of her fruity perfume.

Inspired by the credentials of the gumbo chef, Ara decides to start off at his booth. He charges her four dollars for a foam cupful. 'I don't suppose you'll divulge your recipe,' Ara says demurely, licking her spoon clean. 'This is the best gumbo I've tasted.'

'And have my secret ingredients splashed across the pages of *Le Ti-Cajun Gazette*? Not a chance.'

'Give me a clue,' Ara pleads. 'There's an explosion of flavours in this one little cup.'

'It's a little of this, a little of that. I always throw in something new to surprise the taste buds. The secret is not to be predictable.'

She thinks of Roman's unexpected recovery and decides surprises are not always welcome. 'Let me snap your picture,' she says. 'In case you win.' She pulls the disposable camera from her purse and has the gumbo chef hold up a ladle dripping with his creation. 'Say "unpredictable",' she says.

'Unpredictable!'

She snaps the shot.

'There's some tough competition,' he says. 'Have you tried Bobby Boudreaux's crawfish pie?'

'Not yet,' Ara says. 'I'd better get over there.'

She is slowly coming to the grim awakening that she is nothing but a glorified taste-tester. And she's getting fat. You don't see *real* journalists stuffing their faces with gumbo and crawfish pie in the gymnasium of a local elementary school. She is certain there won't be a Pulitzer Prize at the end of this rainbow.

In the end, the Pillsbury mother wins first prize for her Creole praline pie and Ara doesn't even get a snapshot. The cook-off raises $378. A disappointing turnout by all accounts. Mrs Bouvier blames it on the sagging economy in America. She says, 'Times simply aren't what they used to be.'

Bouvier's grossly inflated perception of herself *and* her grade two cook-off are hilarious, but Ara figures it will make a good quote and give the cook-off story an edge.

Afterwards she makes a Pepto Bismol pit-stop at the Pharmax and then goes back to the office to write up her piece. She includes an interesting profile on the guy who founded the immersion support group, hoping in some small way to weigh down yet another piece of fluff. She headlines it 'Cajuns Cook-Off to Save French Heritage!'

She has learned that an exclamation mark can turn just about any sentence into a decent headline. Add two exclamation marks and you've got a headline worthy of the Watergate scandal.

The Boob is back!!!!

Ara jots that down on a piece of note paper and sends it off to Dayna. She leaves it at that.

A Failure at Meditation

ARA GROPES through her underwear drawer in search of that old black leotard she bought for a short-lived ballet class in the mid-eighties. What she comes across instead is the voodoo doll.

She gasps when she sees it staring up at her with that ghastly face. She picks it up and dangles it over the wastepaper basket for a moment. Then she wonders if perhaps it might be best to burn the damn thing. On second thought, she decides, why rush to dispose of it? Who knows when another opportunity for revenge will arise?

She tucks it back into the drawer, vowing not to use it unless the situation absolutely calls for it – for example, if some tramp breaks Kenny's heart in the future. Otherwise, she won't abuse her voodoo privileges.

After she retrieves the leotard and squeezes herself into it, Ara sits down cross-legged on the floor. She struggles with her left leg, trying to manoeuvre her foot over the thigh of her right leg, but she is unable to arrange herself in yoga position. Her legs just don't move that way. She gives up and rests her hands on her knees with the palms upturned as though to catch raindrops. She closes her eyes.

She concentrates on not thinking. Her *Guide to Daily Meditation* instructs newcomers not to think, but to perceive, to be aware, to focus entirely on the physicality of the moment. The manual suggests paying attention to her breath. At first she can't get past the taste of coffee on her breath, so she goes and brushes her teeth. She settles back into semi-lotus position, closes her eyes and starts *not* thinking all over again. Her breath is much better now, minty fresh. But her tube of toothpaste is almost empty. She makes a mental note to go to the Pharmax tomorrow morning and buy a new tube. She may as well pick up a new deodorant and a box of Q-Tips, too. Kenny has recently developed an obsession with clean ears. She finds his used Q-Tips in the wastepaper basket or floating in the toilet every morning. Boys are peculiar at this age, she thinks. Twelve. If Kenny was Jewish he'd be celebrating his bar mitzvah in a few months. Technically, although not Jewish, Kenny is practically a man. Dayna was easier. Ara was always able to recognize the odd quirks and know what they stood for. She'd lived them herself.

Kenny is handling Roman's awakening with characteristic maturity. He's cautiously pleased but not overly enthusiastic. There wasn't an outburst of emotion when she first told him but then he's never very demonstrative. Now Ara remembers she has to book him a flight back to Montréal. They decided he'll spend Christmas with Roman and she's going to meet Dayna in New York for the holidays. Hopefully there's a connecting flight from Montréal to New York so she can fly with Kenny. She won't feel right if he has to fly alone.

Now she coughs, which startles her away from her thoughts. Oops. She was thinking instead of perceiving. She silently berates herself. Darn, this meditation stuff is hard, she thinks. She tries again, clearing her head and directing all energy to her breath.

Her throat itches. A cold? Bronchitis? There's cough syrup in the medicine cabinet. She'll have a spoonful later, to ward off potential illness. Kenny used to love cough syrup as a baby. Once she caught him drinking it like it was his bottle of orange juice. She had to start locking it up. She misses those days. They were less complicated. The trouble Dayna and Kenny got into as babies and toddlers was far less threatening than the potential trouble that hovers around them now.

'What are you doing, Mom?'

Ara looks up. 'I'm meditating.'

Kenny watches her like she is a strange creature he will never comprehend. 'Don't forget about my date. I have to leave in an hour and thirty-seven minutes.'

'I know. You've been reminding me all day.'

'Should I wear slacks or jeans?'

'If it's a birthday party, you should wear slacks.'

'But all the kids wear jeans.'

'So wear jeans.'

'Okay.'

'Why bother asking me?'

''Cause if you had said jeans, then I would have listened to you.'

Kenny spends the next hour and thirty-seven minutes coordinating a suitable outfit, brushing his teeth, swooshing Scope in his mouth, gargling, cleaning his ears with six separate Q-tips, combing and gelling his hair and removing the lint from his belly-button. (He has an inny, so lint often collects there despite his dedication to personal hygiene.) His primping process amazes Ara. She spent less time getting ready on both her wedding days combined.

When he's finally done, Ara says, 'You look very fresh.'

'Fresh?' Kenny is clearly horrified. He runs back upstairs, rumples his hair, un-tucks his shirt and exchanges his Wallabies for a pair of Nikes. When he comes back down, Ara says, 'Now you look sloppy.'

Kenny smiles.

Rosemary Moncoeur lives in a ritzy part of Lafayette. Her house is one of those Southern plantation-style mansions surrounded by acres of impeccably mowed grass and two willow trees that rustle gently in the breeze. Ara's breath catches as she pulls into the winding driveway. 'It's like Tara,' she says.

'Who's Tara?'

'The mansion from *Gone with the Wind*. It's magnificent.'

'Rosemary is a Southern belle,' Kenny informs her. But when Rosemary darts from her front door to the car wearing baggy jeans, a loose Snoop Doggy Dog T-shirt, combat boots and a backwards baseball cap, she looks more like a gang member than a belle. She throws herself into the back seat. 'Hi, Ken. Hello, Mrs Boot,' she says.

'Hello, Rosemary.' Ara has trouble keeping the contempt from her voice. She scans Rosemary critically through the rearview mirror, searching for budding breasts or any other dangerous signs of womanhood. But Rosemary is thin, flat, still a child. She may shave but body hair is far less threatening than a pair of breasts Kenny might be tempted to bury his face between.

Kenny directs Ara to Mongo Gruber's house on Flatbread Road. 'I'll pick you up at ten,' she says firmly. 'Be waiting outside.'

She watches Kenny and Rosemary saunter up the front walk, ring the doorbell, disappear inside. She wants to run after him, snatch him back, salvage him from whatever unthinkable fate lurks inside. A couples party. The words, seedy and torrid, leave a bad taste in her mouth. She knows she should just turn around and drive home but she feels like she's just dropped Kenny off into the lair of a cult. What if she goes home and they brainwash him over to their side? Teenagers are unpredictable, dangerous. She can't leave her little boy unprotected, especially with that grubby tramp Rosemary.

She decides to sit in her car and wait it out for Kenny's sake so she can be close to him in his hour of need. She decides to clean out her glove compartment, which is full of garbage that dates back a couple of months. She's developed this phobia of throwing things out in public. She's never sure what garbage is supposed to be recycled and what garbage you're still allowed to toss into the trash without reproach. She is especially unsure about foam cups and pop cans, but there is also the problem of paper, which she knows is supposed to be recycled but often she can't find recycling bins and then feels guilty about disposing of the paper in the regular garbage bins. It's complicated in the nineties, she thinks, as she crushes an old coffee cup. You're always at risk of persecution.

Because it's dark outside and the street is deserted, Ara dashes out of the car and dumps all the garbage – paper and Styrofoam included – into a garbage can across the street. She smiles furtively. Sometimes it feels good to break the unwritten rules of society.

Back in her car, she looks at her watch. Two and half hours to go until Kenny is released. She pulls a map from the pocket of her side door and unfolds it. It's a map of Eastern Québec. She traces highway 10 from the red dot that is supposed to be Montréal and follows it through the Eastern Townships, memorizing names of towns like St Angèle-de-Monoir and St Jean-sur-Richelieu. There are a lot of Saints in Québec, she thinks, absently digging around her purse for something to snack on. She finds a loose Lifesaver – butterscotch – and pops it into her mouth.

Her map ends at Vermont, just as it becomes New Hampshire. She took Dayna shopping in New Hampshire at the end of the summer, right before Dayna went off to college. They went to a factory outlet village where Canadians go to buy cheap shoes and Calvin Klein underwear. Dayna bought underwear, hiking boots, a J. Crew sweatshirt, and two scented candles for her dorm room. That New Hampshire town isn't on Ara's map but it's in her memory.

She falls asleep with the map spread out on her lap.

'Mom?'

Ara groans. She is slumped forward with her face pressed against the steering wheel and the corner of the map tickling her nostril. 'Where am I?'

'How long have you been here?' Kenny asks, sliding into the back seat with Rosemary not far behind. 'You didn't stay the whole time, did you?'

Ara gazes out the window. Despite her blurred vision, she can make out Mongo Gruber's townhouse in the distance. And then it comes back to her. The couples party. She jerks around to look at Kenny, to study him for signs of change, damage. He looks the same.

'Mom, you haven't been here all along, have you?'

She shakes her head. 'Of course not. I came a bit early and must have dozed off.'

Kenny looks relieved.

'How was the party?' Ara asks them. What she really wants to know is if there was spin the bottle or make-out sessions or alcohol. It's true they're only twelve, but who knows what kids do these days?

'Fine,' Kenny says. Fine? Fine? What exactly does 'fine' mean, Ara wonders. Fine is a deceitful word, which masks a thousand dirty secrets.

No one says anything until Ara pulls up in front of Rosemary's mansion. Ara watches Kenny and Rosemary carefully to gauge the intimacy level of their goodbyes. But all Rosemary says is, 'See ya Monday,' and 'Thanks for the lift, Mrs Boot,' and runs into her house. Kenny waves indifferently, then climbs into the front seat.

'How was it?' Ara asks, once they are alone and safe. 'What happened? Was there drinking? Kissing? Do you like Rosemary?'

'There was just punch,' he says.

'What about kissing?'

'It *was* a couples party, Mom. Mongo turned the lights off at nine, after the cake, and all the couples had to make out for an hour.'

Ara gasps. 'Did you … ?'

'A little. I didn't want to but everyone else was doing it.'

'And if everyone else went for a swim in the bayou, would you?'

'Rosemary's breath smelled like mushrooms.'

'Mushrooms?'

He nods solemnly. 'It was gross. Like she'd just eaten cream of mushroom soup.'

'Do you like her?'

'She kept saying *ecks*pecially. It was getting on my nerves so finally I told her there's no hard C and she got mad at me for correcting her grammar.'

Ara is secretly pleased.

'She also asked me if I thought she was fat,' Kenny says. 'I told her she was skinny so why would she even ask me that question? She *knows* she's skinny but she kept asking me anyway. Why do girls do that?'

'Because their moms do it.'

'It's dopey.'

'You didn't have fun then?',

'No. Mongo played this techno music all night. It goes boom, boom, boom, boom. He said he wanted his party to be like a rave.'

'What's that?'

'I don't know.'

Ara is very close to gloating. Maybe she's got him for another few years.

'I feel like a hamburger,' Kenny says suddenly.

'A real one? With beef?'

He nods. They go to Jack in the Box and he orders a cheeseburger. After three bites, he runs into the bathroom and throws up.

'Maybe it's too many changes at once,' Ara says gently when he comes back.

'I guess,' he says, sipping on his Sprite. 'I just had a craving.'

'Kenny, was there any tongue?'

'Huh?'

'When you and Rosemary were kissing, was there tongue?'

'She tried to poke hers in my mouth, but I blocked her with my teeth.'

'Good for you, slugger.' Ara finishes his burger with great relief.

War of the Boots

'THERE'S SIMPLY NO JUSTICE,' Ara laments.

'It would have been too easy if he'd stayed in the coma.'

'How do you mean "too easy"?'

'One ex-husband diminished by age and the other a vegetable for the rest of his life? It just doesn't happen that way, Ara. Poetic justice only goes so far. One of them was bound to come back to haunt you.'

Ara pours Gypsi a cup of coffee and refills her own mug. It's Saturday morning and she is still lounging leisurely in her robe and slippers. She's got her hair in rollers and a khaki green mud mask on her face.

'Where's Kenny?' Gypsi says.

'He bought himself a computer. He's upstairs playing Command and Conquer. He barely leaves his room any more.'

'It's better than dating.'

'You're telling me. I'll be happy if he stays in there until he's eighteen. I'm just going to keep buying him new games and programs and sound blowers and CD-rams and whatever else they invent next.'

Gypsi chuckles. 'That's awfully manipulative of you.'

'A woman has to use all the powers she's got available to her,' Ara says. 'You taught me that.'

'I suppose motherhood draws out all of a woman's resources.'

Ara sits back down at the table. 'Any luck with the palm-reading?' she asks.

Gypsi shakes her head. 'Nothing.'

'Miss Potemkin says you might be clogged.'

'Clogged?'

'Yeah. She says a few sessions of psychotherapy will do wonders for your palm reading because it will unclog the drain between your head and your soul.'

'Well, you can tell Miss Drano that psychotherapy is not the solution to *every*thing.'

'How can you be sure?'

'Palmistry has nothing to do with the head, Ara. It's a psychic gift. It's of the spirit. Have you got CoffeeMate?'

'How about cream?'

'I'm watching my weight. Menopause is brutal on the figure.'

The doorbell rings. 'Wonder who that is,' Ara muses, looking over at Gypsi with a puzzled face.

From upstairs, Kenny bellows: '*Mooom*, the doorbell!'

Ara hoists herself up with some reluctance and shuffles languidly over to the front door. Without inquiring who it might be, she generously pulls it open. Her first reaction is outright horror. 'What are *you* doing here?' she gasps. And then her shock dissipates and settles into a somewhat milder disappointment, coupled with the humiliation of being caught after all these months in a green mask with her hair wrapped in rollers.

'Salutations!' Tanya P. chimes, her face lit up by a devious smile. 'I love your new look. Reminds me of Gazoo from the 'Flintstones'! Remember him?'

'Hardy har har,' Ara mumbles.

Roman, slumped in his wheelchair beside her, is as pale and bloated as rising dough. He's wearing a ski tuque over his shaved head, presumably to hide the scar.

'Can we come in?' Tanya wants to know. 'You don't want to leave our little invalid out here all morning, do you?' She glances down affectionately at Roman as though he were her pet; her pet invalid.

Ara steps aside to make room for Tanya to wheel him inside. 'What are you doing here?' she asks again. 'Kenny and I were going to come visit you in Montréal. I was just about to book a flight. I thought it was settled.'

'There's no need for that any more,' Tanya chirps. 'Right, Romy?'

'We are here for Ken-ny,' he stammers.

'What do you mean for Kenny?'

Tanya pats Roman's shoulder. 'Duckie,' she coos, 'don't try to say too much.' Then to Ara: 'We're suing for custody.'

'Hardy har –' Ara says lamely, reaching for the banister to steady herself. 'He's *my* son.'

'Mine too,' Roman bleats.

Ara glances nervously up the stairs towards Kenny's closed bedroom door. She lowers her voice. 'You didn't even like him before Tanya tried to kill you,' she reminds him.

'I was found *not* guilty!' Tanya hisses.

'Let God be the judge of that.'

'You should not have kid-napped my son,' Roman says ever so slowly.

'Kidnapped him?'

'Tan-ya said you kid-napped my son.'

Ara turns to Tanya. 'Why did you brainwash him? What do you have to gain by making him think I kidnapped Kenny?'

Gypsi steps into the hallway then. 'Gypsi!' Ara cries, in a high-pitched, panicky voice. 'This is Roman and ... and ...' she crumbles into sobs before she can even get the name out.

'Tanya,' says Tanya obligingly.

'And this is Gypsi!' Ara wails. 'My spiritual mentor.'

Handshakes all around.

'Roman is accusing me of kidnapping Kenny because Tanya has planted the whole cockamamie idea in his empty head and now they're here to sue for custody!'

'Where is he?' Roman says. 'I want to see him.'

'Can he do this?' Ara asks Gypsi desperately. 'Is this valid?'

'Of course he can!' Tanya pipes in. 'He's the boy's father!'

'Lower your voice, will you?'

Gypsi mulls it over. 'I don't think he has a case,' she says objectively, glaring venomously at Roman. He withers under her cold stare, cowers there pitiously in his wheelchair. 'You *did* commit adultery,' Gypsi points out. 'Or did Tanya here forget to plant *that* in your blank hard-drive?'

'Not to mention Tanya's criminal record,' Ara remarks thoughtfully. 'She did try to kill Roman.'

'It was an accident, a crime of passion,' Tanya prattles. 'B'sides he forgives me, don't you, duckie?'

Roman wipes his forehead. He looks from one woman to the other to the other. The tension is pushing its way through his bulging purple veins.

'My scalp is sweat-ing,' he announces. 'This tuque is i-tchy.'

'I said,' Tanya reiterates firmly, 'don't you forgive me, duckie?'

Again Roman looks beseechingly from Tanya, the lover and attempted murderess, to Gypsi, the wise and intimidating stranger, and finally to Ara, the estranged wife whose life he has come here to destroy. 'A-ra,' he whimpers. 'Come back to me and we will be a fam-i-ly a-gain.'

Tanya swats his frail shoulder with her paw. 'Romy!' she squeals. 'You and *I* are a family now! Remember? *I'm* the one you love. Remember? Right?'

'A-ra,' he pleads urgently. 'Come home.'

'Listen,' Ara says defiantly. 'Let *me* patch up some of those holes in your memory. First off, you did have an affair but it wasn't just the cheating that sent me packin'.'

'What then?'

'I wouldn't know where to begin. The porno thing, for starters.'

'What porno thing?' Tanya and Gypsi chime in at the same time.

'And the way you cared more about your mini-golf tournaments than you did about the kids' school plays and ballet recitals.'

'Day-na took ballet?'

'Kenny did. And you missed every one of his darned recitals!'

'What else?' he sputters.

'It's just *you*,' Ara explains patiently. 'Everything about you gets on my nerves, even that wiry hair that sticks out of your left ear. Even the way your nose droops downward at the tip, and the way you pronounce certain words. It's not "ruf", for crying out loud. It's ROOF.'

'*I* don't mind those things!' Tanya exclaims nobly. 'You're my one and only, Romy-o.'

'Shut up,' he croaks miserably.

Ara, gathering momentum now, continues. 'I don't love you, Roman. You've been a lousy father and an even worse husband. No, wait a minute. You've been a lousy husband and a worse father. Anyhow, I'm an independent woman now and I'm not going backwards.'

'Good for you!' Gypsi applauds. 'Go sister!'

Roman wipes a drip under his nose with the back of his hand. He looks up at Tanya as though resigning himself to a lifetime of her. He sighs dramatically.

'Why don't we ask Kenny who he wants to live with,' Tanya suggests vindictively.

Ara lays a hand over her breast to silence the terrifying pounding in her chest. 'This is nonsense.'

'Then we'll let the court decide for him. I don't mind,' Tanya says lightly. 'I'm on a lucky streak with the judicial system.'

Ara has a moment of total paralysis. What if by some crazy chance Kenny chooses Roman? She would shrivel up from the devastation. Poor Kenny's been waiting a long time for a father; who's to say he wouldn't leap at the chance now?

Tanya has a smug look in her tiny little eyes, which look like blinking Christmas lights against the vast plain of her fat face. Now that her plan is back on track, she's gloating in that vicious, victorious way of hers, the same way she used to at Weight Watchers when she'd drop more pounds in one week than Ara.

'I'll go get him,' Ara concedes softly. She is determined to give Kenny the option, to offer him the possibility of having a father if he wants one. How can she deny him that, when she's the one who up and swept him away?

Now she climbs the stairs feeling nauseous and resigned. There is the wretched, apocalyptic weight of loss in her heart. She resents the showdown. Ignoring the 'Beware of Dog' sign, she knocks on Kenny's bedroom door. The sound of her knuckles against the wood is foreboding to her own ears.

'Come in,' he says distractedly.

'Hey, slugger.'

'Yo, Mom.' He doesn't look up from his computer screen.

'There's someone here to see you.'

'Tell her to go away.'

'Her *who*?'

Kenny swivels around on his chair. 'Isn't it Rosemary?'

'No. Should it be?'

Kenny shrugs. 'She's been pestering me. She writes me love notes in class and stuff.'

'I'll talk to her if you like.'

Kenny laughs out loud. 'Yeah right, Mom! You're so clueless.'

'I am?'

'Don't feel bad. You're a mom.'

'Would it be better if you had a dad right now? You know, to help you deal with girls and puberty and masturbation and –'

He blocks his ears. 'Mom! Ga-awd!'

'Would it be easier if you had a father figure in your life is what I'm asking?'

'How would I know?'

Ara's heart plunges. 'Your father's downstairs,' she says bravely.

'Dad's *here*?'

'He's in a wheelchair.'

Kenny is already dashing out of his bedroom, calling, 'Daddy! Daddy!'

Ara wipes the tears from her eyes and waits there by herself a moment before following his jubilant shrieks down the stairs. When she gets there, Kenny is standing awkwardly in front of his father and there is no sign of Gypsi.

'Where's Gypsi?' she asks with some difficulty. Her face is starting to feel tight from the mask now. She stretches her jaw open to crack it a bit around the mouth area.

'I asked her to leave,' Tanya says. 'This is family business.'

'This is *my* house!' Ara cries helplessly.

'Dad,' Kenny says. 'I went on a date with a girl!'

Roman smiles. 'Good for you, son. What a-bout meat?'

Kenny's fragile face falls. 'I'm still a vegetarian,' he admits. 'I tried a burger at Jack-in-the-Box but ...'

Roman looks disappointed.

'I just couldn't,' the boy says miserably.

'Go on and ask him,' Ara urges Roman. 'Just ask him already, would you?'

'Ask me what?' Kenny says.

'Tan-ya and I want you to come home with us to live.'

'Home?' Kenny says, looking up at his mother nervously. 'Back to Montréal?'

'We sure miss you,' Tanya blandishes.

Kenny scratches his head, perplexed. 'But I live here with Mom.'

'Don't you miss your friends back home?' Tanya asks.

'I didn't have any.'

'How a-bout your old room?' Roman puts in.

'You didn't let me have an aquarium,' Kenny says. 'I have fish now. And a computer.'

'What a-bout me?' Roman says. 'Don't you miss your old dad?'

'Kenny, you don't have to make a decision this minute,' Ara says gently. 'You can think about it.'

'You mean you're making me choose between you?' he whimpers in a small, mortified baby voice.

And the fear reflected back at her in his already too-grown-up face, along with the sudden astounding implication of what they are doing to him – to this sensitive, confused, insecure child – hits her full force like a sharp karate jab to the gut.

'*That's it!*' she barks. 'For heaven's sake, what are we doing to our son? What are we inflicting upon him to serve our own – mostly *your* – selfish purposes? This is any child's nightmare!'

'A-ra –'

She slams her fist on the banister (and regrets it immediately once the throbbing sets in). 'Get out of my house, you selfish cretins!' she roars. 'Both of you are the devil's spawn! I'm gonna make you wish I'd shoved that needle right through the voodoo doll's heart, Roman!'

'Huh?'

They are all staring at her queerly now.

'Well,' she stammers. 'I'm speaking figuratively of course. It's an expression. You know, I'll make you wish I'd shoved that needle right through the voodoo doll's heart, meaning ... don't you go messin' with me, pal!'

Silence.

She perseveres with her tirade. 'I wish she'd done you in with that trophy,' she tells Roman. 'Next time use something heavier, Tanya, like your body weight. That'll finish him off for good!'

Kenny chuckles.

'I won't be bullied around by the two of you any more,' Ara proclaims. 'Now haul-ass out of this house ASAP and if you wish to pursue this, you can talk to my lawyer. I'll see you in court if you're willing to embarrass yourself. I haven't forgotten about the dog collar or the murder charge.'

'What dog collar?' Kenny asks mildly.

'Never you mind. You go on upstairs now. We'll discuss visitation rights later.'

Kenny waves goodbye amiably and scuttles up the stairs. 'Maybe I'll come visit at Christmas,' he calls out, and then disappears.

'His voice is a lit-tle high, isn't it?' Roman remarks. 'He's so ef-fem-i-nate.'

'Out you go,' Ara says impatiently, giving his chair a little push towards the door.

'When did you get so spunk-y, A-ra?'

'It was right around my first orgasm with Hooty,' she answers sublimely.

Roman's eyes twinkle the way they used to right before he popped a video from Rixxxx into the old Betamax. 'You sure got mox-ie,' he says admiringly.

'Listen, my pores feel like cement. I've got to remove this mask.'

Tanya looks down at Roman. 'You're giving up this easy?' she says coolly.

'The gyp-sy was right,' Roman answers. 'We don't have a case. May-be if you hadn't tried to kill me ...'

'Well, if you hadn't screwed that nurse!'

'Dad!' Kenny cries from his hiding spot at the top of the stairs. 'You screwed a nurse?'

'Heavens to Murgatroyd!' Ara groans. 'Get in your room, Kenneth Victor Boot!'

'But Mom –'

'Now! March!'

Kenny stomps off sulkily with a last wave down at his father.

'Maybe I'll take you to the Mad Cow when you visit!' Roman calls up to him. 'May-be you'll try a steak!'

But the boy is already out of earshot.

'I'll make a man of him yet,' Roman vows.

'I hope you'll give me an amicable divorce,' Ara says. 'I don't want a hassle.'

'You've changed,' Roman laments.

'I told you so,' says Tanya. 'She's hardened and bitter.'

'I've simply perfected my character,' Ara informs them. 'I'm gentle inside and strong on the outside. Like I said, I don't want any hassles, but if that's what you're after I'm ready to go to war for my son.'

'You're turn-ing me on,' Roman admits. 'Mr Big is wa-king up.'

'Roman!' Tanya screams, her cheeks turning the purple colour of fury.

'Roman!' Ara screams, repelled and elated and flattered and offended. 'Now take Mr Big and –' she points to Tanya – '*Mrs* Big, and get out of here.'

Defeated, the both of them, they turn quietly and attempt to make a dignified exit, but Tanya's flared denim skirt gets sucked into the wheel of his chair and rips noisily. She fights to retrieve the torn fabric and then hurries away.

Ara looks on, triumphant. Roman may not be a vegetable any more, but then neither is she.

After they leave, she goes into the bathroom and washes off her cracked mask.

Viinde

ARA PICKS UP the Monday *Chronicle-Herald* from her doorstep and carries it inside. She settles down at the kitchen table with a cup of steaming coffee and the paper. She starts on the Jumble, unscrambles the word ORYNJEU, and then doesn't get much farther once Kenny joins her.

'Can I have eggs?' he asks her.

'We're running late,' Ara says. 'Don't you want cereal?'

'Yesterday I had a tummy ache all day from eating Marshmallow Midgets.'

'Then have Sugaroos.'

Kenny sighs and pours himself a bowl of cereal. After breakfast, and after Kenny brushes his teeth and cleans out his ears, Ara drops him outside the Lafayette Middle School. She worries that Rosemary Moncoeur is there in the schoolyard somewhere, waiting to prey on him like a vulture on a carcass, but Ara has to trust that he can fend for himself. Besides, there is always Rosemary's mushroom-smelling breath to keep him from going near her. 'Be careful,' Ara says instinctively.

'I'm just going to school,' he says. 'I'm not going off to Nam.'

He is developing a sense of irony, and a sharp tongue, too. Another bad sign of impending adolescence.

'I'll pick you up at three-thirty,' she says. But he is already gone.

At the *Gazette* office, Ara resumes agonizing over a particularly difficult Jumble word. She is supposed to be editing a stack of copy, but it's the usual boring stuff about this French music festival or that French bake sale.

'Don't you have work to do?' Oliver says, coming up behind her and peering over her shoulder.

'I'm stumped on the Jumble,' she explains. 'I can't get this word. VIINDE.'

'There's someone here to see you, if you can pull yourself away from that damn game.'

Ara spins around in her swivel chair. 'Who?' she says tightly.

'He's downstairs.'

'Who, for heaven's sake?' Her heart feels heavy all of a sudden. 'Is it Roman? Is he in a wheelchair? Darn it, I thought he was gone for good. He called from the airport to say goodbye ...'

'It's Joe "Hooty" Birmingham,' Oliver cuts in. 'Apparently you two really hit it off.' There's something bitter in the way he says this, but Ara doesn't give a damn. She is out of her seat and bounding down the stairs, sweaty palms and heart palpitations nary a concern, before he can finish his sentence.

'Hooty!' she cries, flinging herself into his arms. She inhales the strong smell of Arrid from his pits. Caught off guard, he stumbles backwards into the door. The knob jabs him in the lower back.

'What are you doing here?' she shrieks.

'Can we go for a walk outside?' he asks. 'I sensed hostility from your edituh.'

She nods, grabs her windbreaker from the coatrack in the hall, and leads him outside. 'I've missed you,' she gushes. The trucks on Highway 10 zoom by, rattling the earth under their feet.

'There comes a time,' he says, 'when a man's home can no longer be contained in the case of a saxophone.'

'What are you saying?'

'My heart has been achin', *chère*.'

'For me?'

'Who else?'

'What does this mean, Hoot?'

'It just ain't simple any more, suguh. I try to live in the moment, but the moments are dull, empty. I think my time has come. It's the end of the road. *You're* the end of the road.'

Ara's eyes fill with tears. 'There's a splendid apartment complex on Johnson.'

'Is there a sauna? I always wanted a sauna.'

'We can ask. In the meantime, you're welcome to stay with me.'

'In your suburban split level?'

'With the barbecue on the patio.'

'It'll be hard, you know. Me bein' black an' all. You bein' white.' He pronounces it hoo-ite.

'Nonsense,' she says. 'This is the nineties.'

'It's also the South. Interracial relations are still frowned upon.'

It strikes her as odd, that word. Interracial. It's a talk-show word. A year ago, while still trapped in her dismal marriage to Roman-the-soggy-sandwich-of-men, she never could have imagined herself as part of an interracial romance. Or any romance, for that matter. Hooty does that to her – makes her wonder who she is, who she's become. She suspects that's a good sign. Introspection, she now realizes, should never be a woman's enemy.

'I missed you,' she tells him. 'But I was faithful.' She thinks about Sensei Henry and Oliver, and admittedly it wasn't all that hard.

Hooty touches her cheek. 'You're as magnificent as I remem-buhed,' he tells her.

She brushes the tears from her face and leaves him waiting outside while she confronts Oliver.

He is not at all supportive and barely maintains his civility. 'You slept with an interviewee,' he accuses her. 'You broke the number one rule of journalism: objectivity. That's a no-no at *Le Ti-Cajun Gazette*.'

'I'm very fond of him,' Ara says in defence of her crime.

'What *is* it about him?' Ollie whines. 'What has he got –'

'Don't say it,' Ara pleads. 'I've just been through this with Sensei Henry.'

'I didn't know there was a line-up for your affections.'

'Look, Oliver, he's just Hooty.'

'Hooty-shmooty. I don't get it. He's a seventy-year-old has-been.'

'It's not something you can see on the outside,' she explains. 'So you probably can't understand it. It's just the way I feel when I'm with him. It's an inner thing.'

'Musicians are trouble,' he warns her. 'You'd always be number one with me.'

'*You're* a musician.'

'Not a real one. I just play a few John Denver covers.'

'Ollie, I wish you'd just let go of the fantasy that we belong together.'

'I could fire you for sleeping with our front page story,' he challenges.

'This isn't exactly the *New York Times*. You said so yourself.'

'My ego is bruised. I feel like an imbecile.'

'But you're a fair man.'

'Fair-shmare.'

'He's my soulmate,' she says.

'How do you know?'

'My mentor read it in my palm.'

'He's old enough to be your father.'

'I'd like the rest of the afternoon off,' Ara says.

'You'll miss the singalong.'

'I have to settle Hooty in at my condo.'

Ollie winces. 'What is it about musicians?' he moans.

* * *

That night in bed, with the TV on, Hooty says, 'Even the mundane is romantic when you're in love.'

They are watching *Wanted: In the U.S.A.*

'Would you like another grape?' she asks him.

'Please.'

She pops a seedless green grape from the glass bowl on her belly into his mouth without averting her eyes from the TV. She watches the host, Buck Woods, recite the number of the *Wanted* hotline. He says, 'if you have any information pertaining to this crime, please call 1-800-55-C R O O K.' His voice is deep, hypnotic. She will forever associate his voice with crime.

Then he says, 'Up next, a *Wanted: In the U.S.A.* update. A Mississippi gas station attendant thwarts a young couple who have been spreading terror throughout the South.'

And then a picture of a woman flashes on the screen, with the word APPREHENDED stamped across her face. The woman is Georgia-Rae Pekoe. The man, whose face flashes on screen a moment later, Billy 'Pug' Tibbs.

Ara hands Hooty the bowl of grapes and sits up abruptly. 'I know her!' she exclaims.

'Georgia-Rae Pekoe?'

'She robbed me on the way down here!'

'Wow.'

'Imagine, now she's famous!'

Buck Woods describes the crime spree in graphic detail, recounting every robbery from Mississippi to Virginia and back again. Their modus operandi, says Buck Woods in his deep, ominous voice, hinged entirely on Pekoe's uncanny ability to establish a rapport with the people she would later rob. But gas station attendant Callie Spitnik of Swiftown, Mississippi, recognized her immediately on his way home from work. He picked her up and drove straight to the police station, where her picture was hanging on the wall beside Pug's.

'They might try to contact you,' Hooty says, turning off the TV.

'What for?'

'To testify.'

Ara sighs. 'It's just one thing after another,' she says.

And then the phone rings. 'Mom,' says Dayna, 'are you watching *Wanted: In the U.S.A?* They just caught the woman who robbed you!'

'I know.'

'You might have to testify.'

'I know.'

'When did your life get so exciting?'

'I don't know.'

'Any news from the Boob?'

'He's back in Montréal,' Ara says. 'He called from the airport to say goodbye. I think he's going to give me my divorce.'

'What changed his mind?'

'Tanya. She wants me out of the way so they can have a spring wedding.'

'Woof woof,' Dayna quips. 'Guess what?'

'Hm?'

'I spotted Sly Stallone and Jennifer Flavin outside the St James theatre.'

'Jennifer who?'

'*Mooo*m,' Dayna moans. 'Puh-lease.'

'Are you carrying your mace with you wherever you go?'

'Yep.'

'Keep your keys in your hand at all times, just in case. Sensei Henry told me you can gouge someone's eye –'

'I *know*, Mom.'

'I love you, Danish.'

She hangs up and lets Hooty wrap her up in his arms. He caresses her cheek, then her hair, then lingers down her belly. 'Arabella,' he whispers. 'Ara *bella*.' He says it with an Italian inflection. 'Ara the Beautiful.'

Later when she gets up to brush her teeth, she stares at herself in the mirror of the medicine cabinet. Her hair is growing out slowly, looking less like an old person's hairdo. Maybe she'll try again for that Meg Ryan cut she's been wanting for so long.

She leans forward, inspecting her face up close. She is not searching for new wrinkles or unsightly facial hairs or blemishes like she usually does. This time she is searching for beauty – the beauty Hooty can see.

And she finds it right there in the medicine cabinet mirror!

While she brushes her teeth the word from this morning's Jumble comes to her effortlessly, as though it had been waiting behind the curtain of her consciousness all day for the right moment.

Divine.

An Eric word from her past. A word she has dared not contemplate because of all the dismal memories it shovels to the surface, a word that has carried with it the threat of betrayal for so many years.

Now she reclaims it as her own. She can hear Hooty in the bedroom playing his sax; it soothes him to sleep. She spits out a mouthful of toothpaste suds.

Divine.

Lottery

ARA IS ON STAGE for the first time in her life. She never dabbled in acting like most people do. She never tried out for school plays or got involved with choir or participated in talent shows of any kind. She has basically avoided the stage for as long as she can remember.

And now she's standing on a stage with a TV camera in her face and all of Louisiana might be watching her, not to mention 150 audience members, most of them strangers.

There is a rash all over her neck from nerves, but she planned for it and wore a turtleneck. She fights the urge to scratch in front of the camera. She is so nervous she feels syrupy, barely able to stand up on her own.

'Are you ready to spin the wheel, Ms Boot?'

This is the voice of the *Spin n' Win* host, a middle-aged Monty Hall type with boundless energy and relentless good cheer. He sports a bushy moustache and a full thatch of hair as if a chocolate angel food cake has risen on his head. His suit jacket is too tight around the chest.

Ara gazes out into the audience. The front row contains mostly familiar faces. There are Dayna, Kenny, Miss Potemkin, Gypsi, Sensei Henry, Oliver and Hooty: her children, her masseuse-slash-psychotherapist, her dearest friend, her karate instructor, her boss and her soulmate. A woman doesn't need much more than that in life.

She notices that Oliver, Hooty and Sensei Henry are all sitting side by side, with Hooty in the centre. Ara, not wanting to be a quitter, returned to the dojo and continued with her karate lessons. (It helped that Sensei Henry wouldn't give her a refund. He said it was against the school's policy.) No matter. Ara is now a yellow belt and has managed to forge a solid friendship with the Sensei, who, as it happens, is a very gentle and spiritual man.

His relationship with Hooty and Oliver, however, is somewhat strained. That they are all sitting together is something of a coup; previously, there has been a mixture of contempt and jealousy on all their parts. Ara pretends to be cross with them, frequently admonishing them to behave, as though they were children, but secretly she is pleased to have all three of them fighting over her.

She suspects this satisfaction comes from those desolate years with Eric and then Roman – from a time when her self-esteem was hovering dangerously on the edge of extinction. She hasn't fully recovered from that era, but these things can't be rushed. Gypsi calls it a process.

Ara turns back to the wheel. There are so many prizes to choose from: a trip to Oslo, a grand piano, a furnished RV, a treadmill, and the cash prizes, which range from $5,000 to $500,000.

Ara glances one last time toward the audience. Kenny winks at her.

She reaches for the wheel and pulls down hard, with all the strength she has ever been able to muster. She spins the wheel confidently, knowing that wherever it lands, she can't lose.

MIGUEL CARDINAL

Joanna Goodman's stories have appeared in *B&A Fiction, Event, The New Quarterly* and *The White Wall Review*. In 1996 she was a winner in the Canadian Authors' Association Short Fiction Contest. Her work will also be included in a forthcoming fiction anthology, *A Room at the Heart of Things*, edited by Elisabeth Harvor.

Joanna Goodman recently migrated from Montréal to Toronto.